"No Kissing. That's Part Of The Ground Rules, Rafferty."

He had the temerity to look openly amused. "I'll agree not to kiss *you*. Whether you kiss me, however, is another matter."

She gave him a frosty stare. "I'll do my best to resist."

"So, are we shacking up together?" he asked.

"With an offer like that, how can I refuse?"

"Is that sarcasm I detect?"

"That, and good manners prevent me from saying what else."

He laughed outright then. Her stomach somersaulted and she resisted the sudden strange urge to quell his hilarity with a sultry kiss on his laughing mouth.

Oh, boy, was she in trouble. Until last night, she'd have said that the only way she'd have thought to silence Connor was with an advanced move from her karate class.

Connor was going to be her protector from an unknown threat, but who was going to protect her from the very real threat he represented?

Dear Reader,

Welcome to another scintillating month of passionate reads. Silhouette Desire has a fabulous lineup of books, beginning with *Society-Page Seduction* by Maureen Child, the newest title in DYNASTIES: THE ASHTONS. You'll love the surprises this dynamic family has in store for you...and each other. And welcome back *New York Times* bestselling author Joan Hohl, who returns to Desire with the long-awaited *A Man Apart*, the story of Mitch Grainger—a man we guarantee won't be alone for long!

The wonderful Dixie Browning concludes her DIVAS WHO DISH series with the highly provocative *Her Fifth Husband?* (Don't you want to know what happened to grooms one through four?) Cait London is back with another title in her HEARTBREAKERS series, with *Total Package*. The wonderful Anna DePalo gives us an alpha male to die for, in *Under the Tycoon's Protection*. And finally, we're proud to introduce author Juliet Burns as she makes her publishing debut with *High-Stakes Passion*.

Here's hoping you enjoy all that Silhouette Desire has to offer you...this month and all the months to come!

Best,

Melissa Jeglinski

Melissa Jeglinski
Senior Editor
Silhouette Desire

Please address questions and book requests to:
Silhouette Reader Service
U.S.: 3010 Walden Ave., P.O. Box 1325, Buffalo, NY 14269
Canadian: P.O. Box 609, Fort Erie, Ont. L2A 5X3

Under the Tycoon's Protection

ANNA DePALO

Silhouette®

Desire

Published by Silhouette Books

America's Publisher of Contemporary Romance

SILHOUETTE BOOKS

ISBN 0-373-76643-2

UNDER THE TYCOON'S PROTECTION

Copyright © 2005 by Anna DePalo

All rights reserved. Except for use in any review, the reproduction
or utilization of this work in whole or in part in any form by any
electronic, mechanical or other means, now known or hereafter
invented, including xerography, photocopying and recording, or in
any information storage or retrieval system, is forbidden without
the written permission of the editorial office, Silhouette Books,
233 Broadway, New York, NY 10279 U.S.A.

All characters in this book have no existence outside the imagination of
the author and have no relation whatsoever to anyone bearing the same
name or names. They are not even distantly inspired by any individual
known or unknown to the author, and all incidents are pure invention.

This edition published by arrangement with Harlequin Books S.A.

® and TM are trademarks of Harlequin Books S.A., used under license.
Trademarks indicated with ® are registered in the United States Patent
and Trademark Office, the Canadian Trade Marks Office and in other
countries.

Visit Silhouette Books at www.eHarlequin.com

Printed in U.S.A.

Books by Anna DePalo

Silhouette Desire

Having the Tycoon's Baby #1530
Under the Tycoon's Protection #1643

ANNA DePALO

A lifelong book lover, Anna discovered that she was a writer at heart when she realized that not everyone travels around with a full cast of characters in her head. She has lived in Italy and England, learned to speak French, graduated from Harvard, earned graduate degrees in political science and law, forgotten how to speak French and married her own dashing hero.

Anna has been an intellectual-property lawyer in New York City. She loves traveling, reading, writing, old movies, chocolate and Italian (which she hasn't forgotten how to speak, thanks to her extended Italian family). She's thrilled to be writing for Silhouette. Readers can visit her at www.annadepalo.com.

For my editor, Julie Barrett,
and my friend Vera Scanlon,
for knowing there's a place
in the heart for fairy tales…
and for understanding that
strong heroines write their own tales.

One

Allison Whittaker stared at the man who might be trying to kill her.

She shifted the slats of her window blinds slightly to get a better view of the dark Boston street stretched out below her. The yellowish glow cast by an old-fashioned gas lamp fought a losing battle with the darkness of the cool April night.

The man sat motionless in the driver's seat of the black car across the street, his face in shadow.

He'd been there last night, too.

She'd noticed. She made a point of noticing. More than four years as an Assistant District Attorney in Boston did that to a person. She'd been a lot more naive when she'd been straight out of law school.

A nice genteel white-shoe law-firm job should have been the next rung on the ladder. Her upper-crust family had certainly expected it of her. Her mother, a respected family court judge who'd just had a glowing article written about her in *The Boston Globe,* certainly had.

Instead, she'd surprised them all. She'd gone for the tough prosecutor's job. And not as a prestigious Assistant U.S. Attorney trying federal cases either.

Nope. She'd gone for the down-and-dirty: putting away the friendly neighborhood drug dealer or burglar as a prosecutor in the District Attorney's Office.

She looked down again at the man in the car. Of course, she'd surprise everyone even more if she wound up dead in her apartment, her throat slashed by the mystery man sending her death threats. She didn't want to make that her encore.

She held her breath as the man in the car shifted and opened the driver's-side door.

As he got out of the car, she strained for a better view but couldn't make out his facial features in the dark. What she could tell was that he was tall and solidly built, with sandy-brown hair and dark clothes.

She watched as he scanned the street up and down and then made his way toward the house. Was he heading for her?

Her heart began to pound, her breath catching in her throat. *Call the police!* the rational part of her mind screamed.

Surely the neighbors would hear if he tried to break in? Her exclusive Beacon Hill neighborhood was usually quiet and serene.

The man below passed under a street lamp and her mind pulled the emergency brake on her thoughts.

She knew that face.

Suddenly fear was replaced by anger. Not the simmering variety of anger, either, but a full-blown boil. The type that any of her three older brothers would have recognized as a sign to dive for cover.

She headed for the staircase of the redbrick townhouse that she called home, heedless of the fact that she was dressed for bed in a short silk slip and matching robe. When she got downstairs—the back of her mind taking note of the fact that she hadn't yet heard a knock or bell—she undid the lock on the front door and yanked the door open without ceremony.

"Hello, princess."

Allison felt the same rush of energy she always did in this man's presence, quickly replaced by an undercurrent of pulsing tension.

He had a lithe but muscular physique, one which usually reduced women to giggles and flirtatious banter. But not her. They had too much of a history for that, and she doubted his presence on her doorstep tonight was a mere coincidence.

She crossed her arms and snapped, "Did you take a wrong turn, Connor? The last time I checked, Beacon Hill was too exclusive a neighborhood for riffraff like you."

He had the audacity to look amused, his gaze raking her. "And you're still the perfect diamond blue blood, princess. Just like I remembered."

"If you know anything about diamonds, you'll remember they're the hardest stones around."

"Oh, I know plenty about diamonds these days, petunia," he said, tapping the tip of her nose with his finger as he sauntered inside without invitation, forcing her to take a step back. "I've discovered they're the gift of choice for women in your class."

She yanked her mind from the image of Connor picking out diamonds for his girlfriends. Probably at someplace like the exclusive Van Cleef & Arpels, damn the man. He might have grown up in tough, working-class South Boston, but, thanks to the multimillion-dollar security business he'd started, his bank account was well into eight figures these days. He was quite the self-made tycoon.

She slammed the door shut behind him and locked it. "Make yourself at home." Sarcasm was easier than thinking about him looming in her dark house with no company but her and the turbulent feelings he unerringly evoked in her. "I'm sure you'll tell me in your own good time just what you were doing studying my house in the middle of the night."

"What makes you think I was studying anything?" He peeled off his jacket and tossed it onto a nearby chair.

She rubbed her chin, pretending to contemplate that as she followed him into the living room and watched him flick on a lamp. "Oh, I don't know…could it be the fact that you've been sitting in a car across the street with the engine turned off for the last half-hour?"

She watched as he glanced around the living room. Framed photographs were everywhere, including ones of her with family and friends and holding Samson, her cat who'd died of old age four months ago. She felt vulnerable and exposed, her life on display in so many telling snapshots.

She'd moved into the townhouse after selling her condo last year. Her best friend and sister-in-law, Liz, who was an interior designer, had helped her decorate in an elegant style that fit well with the house's old and patrician history.

He turned back to her. "Nice digs." He bent down and gazed at a picture of her in a bikini on a beach in the Caribbean, laughing back into the camera as she ran with fins and goggles in her hands toward the water. "You filled out nicely, princess, once you finally got through puberty."

She gritted her teeth. Despite the fact that Connor Rafferty had practically become a member of the family since rooming with her oldest brother Quentin at Harvard, she'd never felt comfortable around him. And she'd certainly never thought of him as a brother. Impatiently, she asked, "Why are you here? And more importantly, why were you lurking outside my house so late on a Thursday night?"

He straightened and shoved his hands in his pockets, his jaw hardening. "Did I scare you? Did you think I was that piece of scum who's been sending you those nasty little love notes?"

"No!" She realized a second too late that the vehement denial sounded exactly like the bald-faced lie it was, but his mere presence had set her on edge. She supposed one of her brothers—probably Quentin— had mentioned to him the threats she'd been getting.

He quirked a brow, his tension easing a fraction. "What? Never thought you'd be glad to see me instead?" His lips twisted in wry amusement.

"Get real." In fact, she had been relieved it was him in the split second before anger had stepped in. "And you're evading the question. What are you doing here?"

He walked over and leaned against the back of the chintz-covered couch, his legs stretched out in front of him, feet crossed. "Just doing my job."

"Just—" She stopped as an unwelcome thought intruded and her eyes narrowed.

He cocked his head. "You were always a quick study, petunia. Though, I have to confess, it is fascinating to watch those wheels turn in that devious little head of yours. I've always said that if you'd been born a redhead, the package would have been perfect. Red hair to match that red-hot temper of yours."

"Get out."

She watched his eyes narrow and his lips set in a firm line. "Now is that any way to treat the guy who's here to protect you?"

She strode into the room and whirled back toward him once she got to the fireplace. She couldn't believe this was happening. "I don't know which member of my family hired you, Connor—" she said, crossing her arms "—and, frankly, I don't care. You may own the best security firm in the country, but you're not wanted or needed here, got it?"

Pushing away from the couch, he folded his arms, looking as easy to move as a boulder up a mountain. "Based on what I've heard, I'd say I'm definitely needed around here. As to whether I'm wanted—" he shrugged "—I've been asked to do a job and it's going to get done."

Want. Her mind zeroed in on that one word, then quickly backed away. Whatever she felt for Connor, *that* certainly wasn't an apt description.

True, with hazel eyes framed by long, thick lashes and sandy hair cut conservatively short, he was model material except for the nose that had been broken a couple of times and the crescent-shaped scar marring his chin. But in her mind that was all overshadowed by the fact that he was condescending and annoying. Not to mention an untrustworthy snitch.

She hadn't seen him since her brother Quentin's wedding a few months back, but though their paths hadn't crossed much lately, he was as familiar to her as a member of her family. He, on the other hand, hadn't really had family to speak of, having lost both parents by the time he'd gotten to Harvard. Instead, he'd spent most school holidays with the Whittakers.

She placed her hands on her hips. "There's no way you can do this job if I'm telling you that you *can't*."

He rubbed his chin, seeming to contemplate that for an instant. "Since Quentin still owns this place—" he nodded around him "—because you haven't gotten around to closing the deal with him yet to purchase it, I'd say you're wrong about that. So, first thing we're going to do is make sure that security at the bachelorette pad is up to snuff."

The familiar urge to throttle Connor Rafferty was coming over her again. True, she didn't own the townhouse, but that was a mere technicality. The house had stood empty for two years after Quentin had purchased it as an investment, but she'd fallen in love with it and offered to buy it from him. In any case, she didn't need a bodyguard. "If I need protection, *I'll* get it."

His lips thinned, his gaze holding hers. "That won't be necessary, because I'm planning to stick to you like Krazy Glue until we get to the bottom of who's been sending you death threats in the mail and spray-painting obscenities on your Mercedes."

"I can take care of myself. I spotted you lurking around outside in a parked car, didn't I?"

The thin line of his lips curved upward in a humorless smile. "What about that guy who was in the parked car at the street corner? Don't tell me you missed him?"

She had.

He raised an eyebrow, seeming to read her silence for the admission it was.

"You can't be sure that was in any way connected to me." She knew she was right, nevertheless her heart tightened.

"You're right, I can't. But he was out of there like a speeding bullet as soon as I decided to test my theory by getting out of the car."

"And you didn't go after him?"

He shrugged. "How could I be sure he was after you?" he asked, tossing her words back at her.

At her impatient look, he added, "Anyway, it was too late to get back in the car to follow him and I couldn't make out his plate number or even the make of the car in the dark before he disappeared. So, instead, I came to your door thinking at least I'd get thanked by the damsel in distress for running off the bad guy."

"Now that you've run him off, would you mind running off yourself?" Even if she needed protection, she could arrange for it herself. The last thing she needed was a bodyguard hired by her overprotective family, not to mention one as distracting and annoying as Connor was.

His brows drew together. "You really don't get it do you, princess?"

She pretended to look bored. "I suppose you're going to explain so I can 'get it.'" She stood her ground as he strode toward her. If he thought to intimidate her, he had another thing coming.

"You suppose right." He stopped mere inches away.

She had to tilt her chin up to keep eye contact with him and caught the muscle ticing in his jaw. She ought to take perverse satisfaction in knowing that, as much as he unsettled her, she seemed to have an uncanny ability to annoy him as well.

"Working for the DA's Office these days may give you the idea that you're streetwise," he growled, "but you're not." He looked her over. "Which leads me to wonder why you didn't stick with what all the other debutantes and society ladies do for public service?

You know, organizing a charity auction or something. Why bother working with the tough guys at the DA's Office?"

She gritted her teeth and prayed for patience even though outrage bubbled up inside her. "This isn't a hobby. It's a career."

She knew he'd had a rough childhood on the sometimes unforgiving streets of South Boston, but, really, that didn't give him the right to constantly tweak her nose about having grown up with a silver spoon in her mouth. After all, he didn't play the wealth card with Quentin.

Connor's eyes narrowed. "You've made a career out of looking for a thrill, haven't you, petunia? I've wondered why that is and why you can't seem to get what you want with the pampered trust-fund boys over at the country club."

She glanced around for something to throw, then decided it would be a pity to waste some heirloom against his hard head. And, besides, she'd be playing into every preconception he had of her. "So sure you know it all, don't you? Except, guess what? I'm no longer some teenaged kid that you can rat out to her parents."

He looked at her assessingly, his hazel eyes darkened to a nearly amber color. She could tell from the flare of his nostrils that he had his temper on a very short leash. "Still can't forgive me for that one, can you?"

She arched a brow and ignored the way his near-ness was coaxing every surface cell in her body into oversensitized awareness. "Don't flatter yourself."

He had the height advantage by a good six inches over her five-foot-eight frame, but she was used to holding her own against three brothers who similarly bested her. "Saying that I can't forgive you implies I still care about what happened, which I don't."

His lips thinned. "Yeah, and you haven't seemed to have learned a lesson from it either."

"Oh, I learned," she countered. "I learned I couldn't trust *you*."

"You were a naive seventeen-year-old kid who'd started hanging out with the wrong crowd. What did you think? That biker boy in that bar was coming on to you because he wanted to take you home to share a root beer?"

"And you weren't my keeper!" She didn't add that one of the reasons she'd been in the bar that night was because she'd been hoping *he* would turn up. She'd briefly—very briefly—in her teenaged years had what some might have called an infatuation for Connor. But that was before he'd proven, by betraying her faith in him, that he'd seen her only as a pesky kid.

She could still recall the waves of embarrassment and humiliation she'd felt when he'd dumped her over his shoulder in the bar and marched out to his car, heedless of her kicking and yelling.

As if that weren't enough, despite promising her that, if she kept still, he wouldn't give a full report to her parents, he'd gone ahead and ratted her out anyway. She'd gotten a long lecture about underage drinking and sex, been grounded for a month, and had her comings and goings forever questioned after that.

Aloud, she said, "I'd say you're just as guilty as I am, Connor, of not learning lessons from the past. You're still acting like my keeper when you're not."

He finally seemed to be pushed over the edge. "Dammit! Are you so stubborn that you won't accept help even when you need it? When your life may be in danger?"

"Stubborn?" She tilted her head to the side. "Seems to me you could write a magnum opus on that subject."

She started to brush past him but he grabbed her arms and forced her gaze to his. His expression was stormy, his brows drawn together and his lips compressed. "Stubborn, thickheaded…"

She braced her hands against his chest. "Likewise," she retorted. They were practically nose to nose, and beneath the adrenaline pumping through her veins, a little thrill of excitement intruded at having finally shaken his control—his *years-old* control.

His head swooped down then, cutting off her gasp of surprise as he seized her lips in an angry kiss. His lips moved over hers with hard pressure, and, when she would have jerked away, his hand came up to the back of her head to anchor her in place.

"Mmm…!"

Back when she'd been seventeen, she'd often daydreamed about what it would be like to be kissed by Connor Rafferty. But none of the scenarios had been like this. He kissed the way he did everything: with a cocky confidence that took no prisoners.

When he finally pulled away, their breathing was rapid as their eyes met. His hazel ones held a challenge, as if he was daring her to make some flippant comment about what he'd done and what invisible line had been crossed.

Her mouth opened, but when his gaze shot downward and narrowed, she clamped her lips together again. The tense moment stretched between them. She was acutely aware of how close he was, of the leashed energy emanating from him.

And then, without knowing exactly how and why it happened, she was in his arms again and his lips were on hers in an instant and she was responding the way she used to dream about, except now she could do a little real-life comparison.

His lips, for one thing, were softer and smoother than they looked. They slid over hers, molding and caressing, coaxing a response. His hands didn't roam, instead they exerted a subtle pressure between her shoulder blades and at the middle of her back.

He didn't make a sound, but focused all his concentration on giving and receiving pleasure from the stroke of his lips against hers. Whereas his first kiss had been angry, this one seduced.

Her lips parted beneath his and his tongue slid inside her mouth to stroke against hers, inviting her to respond. The evening shadow that darkened his jaw was a rough caress against her soft skin.

He pulled her closer, flush up against him, as she was caught up in the rush of feeling that had burst between them.

She might have been able to chalk up the first kiss as a fluke, but this second kiss…well, Connor Rafferty was the best kisser behind the best lips she'd ever encountered—and that included Ben Thayer in high school, who'd read and mastered *100 Creative Kisses: Smooching with Confidence.*

When his hand slid down and cupped her bottom to pull them closer together so their bodies were in intimate contact, alarm bells went off in her head. She grasped his shoulders, intent on pushing him back, when she realized the ringing wasn't only in her head.

The phone rang again, insistently, and Connor set his hands on her shoulders to steady her as they broke apart.

Flustered, she glanced around the living room to determine where the ringing cordless was located.

She spotted it peeking from under a throw pillow on the couch and hesitantly picked it up. "Hello?" Her voice was still husky with arousal.

"I'm coming for you." The voice at the other end of the line was raspy and hoarse.

"Who is this?"

"Lay off your cases at the DA's Office or you'll end up dead."

Her hand tightened on the receiver. She knew she had to keep him talking to get more clues. "I don't scare easily."

Out of the corner of her eye, she saw Connor tense and his brows draw together. She turned away as he strode toward her.

There was a grim chuckle on the phone line. "I'm willing to bet Daddy would pay a nice little sum to get you back—dead or alive."

Suddenly, the receiver was torn from her hand. "Touch her and I'll obliterate you like the scum you are." Connor's voice was clipped and deadly. "You won't be able to walk down the street without watching your back."

Allison guessed the line must have gone dead because Connor punched a few buttons on the receiver, listened for a few seconds, and then tossed the phone onto a chair with a disgusted look on his face. "Should have known it wouldn't be that easy to trace."

"Why did you do that?" she demanded, bracing her hands on her hips. "You didn't even give me a chance to try to draw him out."

"Draw him out?" he asked incredulously. "Forget it, honey. You may work for the DA, but take it from someone who's had a lot more experience with criminals. This guy's a wily bastard. He's only going to be drawn out when he comes for your pretty little neck."

"There's no need to be crude," she snapped.

"What did he say?" he demanded.

"He warned me to back off the legal cases I'm working on."

"And?"

"And what?"

"What else?"

Seeking a distraction, she adjusted a pillow on the couch. "And he implied that kidnapping was in the cards." She didn't add the part about a ransom to get her back—dead or alive. No use adding even more fuel to Connor's bonfire.

Two

Connor cursed. "I'm bunking down here."

"What?"

"You heard me. My job starts now." He cast a skeptical look at her tiny, chintz-covered couch. It looked about as comfortable as a linoleum floor. "I don't suppose that couch converts into a sofa bed?"

"It doesn't convert into anything. It's an antique."

He could almost hear her mentally add, "And if you'd grown up with some class, you would have known that."

In his line of work, he'd become accustomed to spoiled, born-rich types who looked down their noses at him and the shadings of a Boston accent that still caused him to drop his *r*'s on occasion.

He'd long ago mentally filed Allison Whittaker under the heading Pampered Debutante. In return, she treated him with a haughty disdain that was so cool it could give polar bears frostbite.

True, he'd long ago sparked her ire by hauling her butt out of that rough-and-tumble bar, but he'd been fully justified. She'd been too much of a sheltered and naive princess to know what she was getting herself into.

When she'd announced after law school that she was joining the District Attorney's Office, he'd figured she'd last about a nanosecond. She'd surprised him by hanging on for four years, but he'd always thought—despite his taunt about her aversion to the country-club crowd—that it was only a matter of time before she threw in the towel to marry a guy named Sloan, or, God forbid, Blake, and raise little Ralph Lauren-clad infants in an upscale suburb.

He glanced at the clock on the mantel. Since she looked ready to argue with him again, he decided to change tactics. "It's nearly two in the morning. I'm beat and in no mood to drive back to my place. So, why don't you show some mercy here?"

He watched the fast-moving emotions on her face as she debated what to do. When she seemed to come to a conclusion, he knew he'd won, but he carefully schooled his features into a bland expression.

"Fine," she said reluctantly. "But only for tonight." She moved toward the doorway. "There's a guest bedroom. I'll just go up and make sure it's in shape."

As he watched her leave, he figured he'd deal with the morning when it arrived. Allison was in over her head here, and, whether she wanted to admit it or not, she needed him.

He moved around the room restlessly. He'd gotten a call that morning from Allison's brother Quentin. Naturally, all the Whittakers were concerned that Allison was being harassed and that it might be connected to one of her cases at the District Attorney's Office. But Allison—not being one to be cowed easily, a trait he normally would have admired—had insisted she could handle matters by herself and no one should overreact.

His natural reaction had been to volunteer his security services. And, because Quentin was an old friend and the Whittakers had been good to him, he'd insisted on taking this matter on personally—with no fee.

He hadn't divulged *that* to Allison, of course. He figured it would be easier if she thought he was a hired hand rather than some quasi–big brother trying to step in and do the right thing.

And the truth of the matter was, whatever he felt these days, he was damn sure it wasn't brotherly. True, she drove him nuts, not the least because of her open disdain for him. But, as much as it irked him, they hit sparks off each other whenever they were in the same room.

He had enough sexual experience to recognize that for what it was. The signs were all there and too obvious to ignore. He was acutely aware of her—the light, flowery scent that clung to her skin, the startlingly brilliant blue of her eyes, the thick mass of dark-brown hair cascading past her shoulders.

She was curvy, too, her nicely rounded figure making her neither voluptuous nor willowy, but just right for making his body tighten whenever he was around her. He'd nearly blown a fuse when she'd opened the door in that short and silky slip, its matching robe gaping open above its loosely and obviously hastily tied belt.

He shoved his hands in his pockets. If he didn't watch it, he'd get aroused right now, just thinking about her, and he couldn't afford another lapse.

The long-simmering kettle of tension between him and Allison was getting harder to ignore and living with her under the same roof was going to try his self-control to the limit.

He'd *kissed* her, for cripes' sake. Sure, he might try to rationalize it, but he knew the truth was more complicated than that.

What's more, she'd kissed him back. Now *that* was an interesting little reaction for him to puzzle over. She'd been all fiery passion, just as he'd thought she'd be, and he, Lord help him, had been more than ready to be consumed by the heat.

He wondered what would happen if he tried to kiss her again…. He started to grin, then stopped short. *Get a grip, Rafferty. You're here to protect her.*

True, Allison had grown from a pesky kid into a beautiful, desirable woman. But they didn't get along well enough for anything longer than a fling, and anything shorter would feel as if he were betraying his friendship with the Whittakers. And that went a long way toward explaining why his attraction to Allison had lain dormant, never acted upon—until tonight.

So, protect her he would, his raging hormonal re-action to her be damned. Just thinking about some-one trying to harm Ally had made his blood boil. She might send his libido into overdrive, but she also had some jerk trying to spook her.

Fortunately, he'd been able to persuade her to let him spend the night at her place. But bigger battles lay ahead. She thought she was getting rid of him this morning, but she had another thing coming.

In the morning, Allison dressed for work and got downstairs only to discover Connor was already in the kitchen, dressed in last night's form-fitting black jeans and white T-shirt—which, to her chagrin, out-lined the lean but hard-looking muscles of his chest.

He looked up from tossing a pancake and nodded toward the coffeemaker. "Help yourself."

She guessed she wasn't getting rid of him just yet. She didn't have it in her, however, to be irritated about it. "Thanks for making breakfast." The aroma of the coffee and the smell of pancakes were already seducing her taste buds.

His lips quirked up, as if in acknowledgement that her statement was dictated only by good manners. "You're welcome." He slid a pancake onto a waiting plate. "I never leave the house in the morning without a shot of carbs," he added, as if by way of explanation for his presence in her kitchen.

When they'd almost finished breakfast, she decided to tackle the bear in the room that they were both ignoring. "The threats are ridiculous. I mean, whoever is making them has to know that even if he gets me off my cases, they'll still go forward. The DA's Office will just get another prosecutor to handle them."

Connor took his time answering, wolfing down the last of his pancakes. "That's true. But no one knows your cases as well as you do. Whoever is threatening you is probably betting the DA's case will be a lot weaker with a prosecutor who has been substituted midstream."

"But that's crazy!"

"Yup." Connor nodded. "Crazy and desperate."

Was he purposely trying to scare her?

As if reading skepticism on her face, he continued, "There've been plots in the past to knock off judges. A defendant may figure he can get a more sympathetic judge if he succeeds in getting rid of the first one." He shrugged. "It isn't a big leap to think someone's guessed a similar strategy could work with an overzealous Assistant DA."

She felt a prick of annoyance. "I'm not overzealous."

Connor leaned back in his chair. "Yeah, but you're doing your job too well and it's scaring this guy. When I called you overzealous, I was just conjecturing about what our Mr. Nice on the phone could be thinking—and what might be motivating him. Maybe the next Assistant DA won't care as much about your cases or won't have your determination and brains."

She couldn't help the frisson of happiness that went through her at his offhand compliment.

Connor leaned forward and shoved his empty plate aside. "Is there one case you've been working on a lot?"

She gave him a sardonic look. "I only wish there was just one." She knew she should be standing up right now, thanking him for his concern and showing him to the door, just as she'd promised last night. Yet, she supposed, she owed him some satisfaction in return for his concern, however misplaced, not to mention for cooking breakfast.

"All right, what's *a* major case you're working on?"

She considered a moment, then said, "One of them is the Taylor burglary case."

"That one hasn't made the papers."

She nodded. "It wouldn't, but Sam Taylor has a rap sheet that's long and interesting, including drug dealing and misdemeanor assault and battery. This time he's charged with burglarizing a home."

"Is he out on bail?"

"No, he's behind bars awaiting trial." Then she added, by way of explanation, "He's only in his early twenties, so there's still time for him to move on to more serious crimes even if he gets off for this one— or even if he doesn't but gets out of prison in a few years."

Connor nodded curtly. "Drug dealing. Was he a neighborhood pusher?"

"Basically."

Connor drained his coffee cup, taking his time asking his next question. "Has anyone linked him with a gang? He's the right age and corner-dealing is the bread-and-butter of gang business."

His perceptiveness surprised her. "Some of his neighbors have more or less said so. Off the record."

His face gave away nothing. "So, some gang members may be harassing the Assistant DA who's trying to put their old buddy Taylor in the slammer for a long while."

A chill went through her as he gave voice to the fear that she refused to acknowledge, but she forced herself to nod in agreement. "All right, I buy that logic."

"Any other prosecutions you're handling?"

"There's the Kendall case."

"Okay, what's the Kendall case?"

She shrugged. "Business executive accused of embezzlement. Part of it is what accountants know as a lapping scheme. Basically, stealing and then hiding the fact by applying subsequent revenue to cover the missing money in the company's accounts receivable." She paused. "At least that's what we're trying to prove."

"Kendall. Name sounds familiar."

She nodded. "He's high profile. Sits on a bunch of charitable boards. A big social climber."

His lips twisted. "Great, my favorite type."

She pasted a look of mock surprise on her face. "What? You dislike the social climbers as much as the born-rich types? Are there any types you *do* like?"

He gave her an inscrutable look before mentally seeming to shift gears back to the issue at hand. "Those white-collar crimes often settle. Just the thought of landing in a cell next to your run-of-the-mill burglar or drug dealer is usually enough to get these guys' defense attorneys to talk settlement."

"True, but, in this case, Kendall doesn't want to

admit any wrongdoing." She was surprised by Connor's knowledge of law enforcement. She supposed she really shouldn't be though. His father had been a cop and Connor had in all likelihood worked with the police and prosecutors on numerous occasions on behalf of his clients.

She added, "As I said, Kendall is a social climber. If he's convicted, it'll ruin him. Right now his public relations firm is spinning this as the DA's Office's misguided attempt to bring down one of Boston's big philanthropists."

"Is Kendall out on bail?"

"Yes."

"Okay, so Kendall is free to come and go. Unlike Taylor, who could, despite that, have some buddies on the outside helping him out. On the other hand, Kendall appears to be just a white-collar criminal. We don't know whether he has it in him to get his hands dirty with death threats."

She gave him a look of studied patience. "In other words, I'm working on two major cases, so I have two defendants with motives to do me wrong? Is that what you're saying?"

He quirked a brow. "What I'm saying is, put a lid on it, petunia. Someone's after you and we haven't answered the who, what, and why questions yet. Until we do, it's best if I stay here."

Stay here? Hadn't they settled this last night? *He*

was going, going, gone. In fact, he should have been gone already. If she wasn't such a sucker for coffee—not to mention pancakes for breakfast—she'd have seen him out the door an hour ago. In any case, there were so many things wrong with his suggestion she couldn't begin to count them.

"You can't stay here." She added a note of finality to her tone.

"Can't?"

"It's not necessary." She added repressively, "I thought we'd settled this last night."

He glanced around in disgust. "Wake up, princess. You don't even have an alarm system around here."

"I'll have one put in."

He said dryly, "That's exactly why I was hired." Then added, "But putting in a security system takes time. Even a company like Rafferty Security needs a few days to do a job like this."

She should have seen this coming the minute she got downstairs to find him flipping pancakes. The sneak. "So, I'll stay with…" Who? She searched her brain in a hurry. Her parents? One of her brothers? The options weren't enticing. "My parents."

"Your parents live in Carlyle. That's going to be quite a commute." He folded his arms over his chest and sat back, apparently digging in for battle. "And, let's see…" He snapped his fingers. "Oh yeah, if I were a criminal trying to kidnap you, I'd absolutely love the chance to follow your car home from the office on a deserted road at one o'clock in the morning."

"One of my brothers then. Quentin, Matt and Noah all keep apartments in Boston."

"They're often not even *in* Boston. Ever since he got married, Quentin has settled down to domestic bliss in Carlyle with your friend Liz and their baby. And Matt and Noah are often on the road for Whittaker Enterprises. If you disappeared from one of their apartments, no one would discover it for hours, even a day or two."

She knew he was right, but she rebelled at the thought. No one, least of all her family, seemed to understand that a bodyguard would raise eyebrows at the DA's Office. She'd worked too hard at her career to have her credibility undermined by the poor-little-rich-girl image that had stalked her her entire life.

Connor unfolded his arms. "What you need is a bodyguard," he stated matter-of-factly. "But I understand why that might be a problem for someone in your position."

"Thanks," she said wryly, his perceptiveness taking her by surprise. "At least you're more reasonable than my family."

"So," he went on, "that's why I'm suggesting another option. Namely, me. All anybody else needs to know is that I'm a friend of the family who's moved in with you for a while, maybe until renovations on my own place are done."

The man had a stubborn streak a mile wide. Even if he did manage to keep a lower profile than a typical bodyguard, his offer was unwise. Very unwise if last night's kiss was anything to judge by. "I thought we'd been over this. No."

"I'll pick you up and drop you off at work," he continued unperturbed, "and, as an added bonus—" he gestured to their surroundings "—I'll stay here with you."

"How magnanimous of you."

He gave her a humorless smile. "Don't worry. I'm house-trained and basically pick up after myself."

She rolled her eyes.

He leaned in then, suddenly serious, his hazel gaze capturing and holding hers. "This isn't a game, Allison. Someone has already vandalized your car and sent you death threats. You don't know what he'll do next."

"I know." She'd tried not to focus on the danger but, instead, on finding the perpetrator. She refused to live her life in fear—although, truth be told, hadn't that been part of her motivation last night for being at the window, peering down at a dark street?

Connor continued, "Your family said the police are involved, but you and I both know those resources only go so far."

She'd always known Connor Rafferty was a man who didn't take no for an answer. He was, after all, the guy who'd climbed out of South Boston and, by the age of thirty-seven, had built a multimillion-dollar enterprise offering security systems and personal protection to big companies as well as the rich and famous.

But, she reminded herself, he was also the guy who'd hauled her teenaged butt out of a dark bar over ten years ago. The guy who still acted at times as if she were a pesky little kid, regardless of last night's inexplicable kiss.

Fortified by that thought, she tried again for a polite brush-off. "Look, Connor, I appreciate the offer, but, as you just said, the police are on it. The DA's Office also has detectives assigned to it."

His eyes narrowed. "And what if I said you really don't have a choice in the matter?"

She scoffed, then stopped abruptly as he reached into the pocket of his jeans and pulled out a set of house keys. Alarm bells went off in her head. "Where did you get those?"

"When I'm hired for a job, I usually get access to the premises," he said coolly.

She pursed her lips. She knew exactly which Whittaker to thank for giving him access. When she was through with Quentin, his ears would be ringing for days. In the meantime, she had one cagey security expert to deal with.

Quite clearly, she wasn't simply going to be able to banish Connor as she'd like. Experience had taught her, however, that it was better to graciously call a temporary truce rather than to admit defeat. She needed time to figure out how to get him out of her house. In the meantime, she'd play along with his game.

"I see," she said, keeping her voice a few degrees cooler than his. "Well, if you're going to be my temporary roommate, then we should set some house rules."

"Such as?" His tone was suspicious, wary.

"Last night was a mistake that will not happen again, got it? Unfortunately, you caught me at a weak moment, when my defenses were down."

"That's the idea."

She narrowed her eyes. "As I said, it will not happen again."

"Are we, by any chance, talking about the kiss we shared?"

"Of course I'm talking about the kiss." Somewhere in the last few hours, the kiss—really two kisses that had seemed to flow almost seamlessly together—had assumed a singular identity all its own, so that she now referred to it mentally as "The Kiss."

"Just checking," he said in a voice that was so amiable it set her teeth on edge.

"And let me correct you, it's not 'the kiss we

shared.' It's the kiss that you planted on me when I was distracted and vulnerable."

His lips teased upward on one side. "Funny, you seemed to have enjoyed it."

"No kissing. That's part of the ground rules, Rafferty."

He had the temerity to look openly amused. "I'll agree not to kiss *you*. Whether you kiss me, however, is another matter."

She gave him a frosty stare. "I'll do my best to resist."

"So, are we shacking up together?" he asked.

"With an offer like that, how can I refuse?"

He broke into a grin. "Modesty prevents me from saying more."

"I've always said it's your strong suit."

"Is that sarcasm I detect?"

"That and good manners prevent me from saying what else."

He laughed outright then, his eyes crinkling at the corners. Her stomach somersaulted and she resisted the sudden strange urge to quell his hilarity with a sultry kiss on his laughing mouth.

Oh boy, was she in trouble. Until last night, she'd have said that the only way she'd have thought to silence Connor was with an advanced move from her karate class.

At least until she could figure out how to get rid

of him, Connor was going to be her protector from an unknown threat, but who was going to protect her from the very real threat he represented?

Three

Connor's suspicions were immediately roused when Allison didn't argue about his insistence on driving her to work. His instincts told him she was far too docile. She was up to something, but he wasn't sure what.

Nevertheless, he didn't dwell on it because he had a typical jam-packed work day ahead of him, starting with driving back to his condo to change into a business suit before heading to Rafferty Security's headquarters.

At lunchtime, he drove over to Whittaker Enterprises' headquarters in Carlyle. He and Quentin had long ago scheduled lunch at Burke's Steakhouse for today. They tried to fit in a lunch appointment from time to time, often at Burke's, as a way of keeping in touch despite their busy schedules. He knew, however, that this time Quentin would have questions about how things were going with beefing up Allison's security.

He hadn't been wrong, he thought, as he shifted in the seat he'd taken in front of Quentin's desk because they still had a few minutes before they had to walk over to Burke's.

"I tried to talk to her about taking some more safety measures," Quentin was saying, "but she just shrugs me off. Tells me she's dealing with it. But, the thing is, she's in a high-profile job and coming into contact with unsavory types every day."

Connor nodded. "I'm doing my best. She wasn't exactly thrilled to see me last night." He added wryly, "And, you know, I'm not known for my ability to be charming and ingratiating."

Quentin chuckled. "Yeah, but I haven't got a choice…"

The door to the office swung open and Quentin's voice trailed off as Allison strode in.

Her clear, sky-blue eyes flashed her annoyance. "Are you two discussing me, by chance?"

She was dressed in the navy suit that Connor had seen her in that morning, the open collar of her white shirt giving a tantalizing glimpse of her bare throat.

Her high-heeled black leather pumps set off her shapely legs beneath her short skirt.

The mere sight of her awakened every male need Connor had, but she had completely disregarded everything he'd said this morning.

Quentin muttered a curse under his breath. "I suppose Celine let you come right in, didn't she?"

"Actually, your secretary stepped away from her desk right after letting it slip that you were meeting with Connor." Connor watched as Allison's eyes settled on him then, a disdainful look on her face. "I might have known you'd be here. Patting yourself on the back for a mission accomplished, are you?"

He rose from his seat. "I'll only feel a sense of accomplishment once we track down the guy who's after you." Sternly, he went on, "I thought I told you to stay put and that I'd pick you up from the office when you were ready to leave."

"Yes, I do recall you ordering me to stay put. What I don't recall is my agreeing to it, especially since I have my dear sibling to thank for my new living arrangements." She folded her arms and sat on the corner of Quentin's desk, glancing back at her brother, who merely raised an eyebrow inquiringly at her.

"Hello, Quentin," she said coolly. "Just the person I wanted to see. You know, the last time I checked, tenants still had the right to peaceful occupation of the premises without unwanted roommates being foisted on them." She fixed her brother with a hard stare. "So far I've resisted the urge to file a complaint against you with landlord-tenant court. I know that would break Mom's heart."

"Is that what you came here to do? Complain?" He added in exasperation, "And, for the record, what would break Mom's heart is if we found you dead in a ditch. We're all worried sick about you and this psycho who's sending you threats."

"Well, of course Mom is worried!" Allison retorted. "She was also worried when Noah took up race-car driving a few years ago. When Matt decided he'd try rock-climbing. And, when *you* went backpacking through Europe. *But* she trusted you to take precautions."

Quentin leaned forward. "What's wrong with getting a little help in this case? I couldn't even mention Connor's name without you going ballistic on me." Quentin folded his hands on his desk. "Connor is the best in the business. The only reason you won't consider him is that you two do nothing but snap and bark at each other."

"Great, won't that make us pleasant roomies!"

Connor gained grim satisfaction from the thought that she sounded worried about their living situation. "I can stand the heat in the kitchen if you can, petunia."

She gave him the imitation of a smile. "You won't

need to worry about the kitchen, Connor, because I plan to light a fire under you."

Their gazes locked while Quentin stifled a laugh. Connor wondered what she'd say if he told her she'd already lit a fire inside him. He'd just been unsuccessfully dousing the flames for years.

Quentin cleared his throat. "If you think I'm meddling, Ally, just consider it payback for your meddling in my life. That was a nice little performance last year, orchestrating to throw me and Elizabeth together."

"That was different."

Quentin's expression showed skepticism. "Oh, yeah?"

Connor knew that, partly thanks to Allison's machinations, Quentin and her best friend Liz were now married and the parents of one-month-old Nicholas.

Allison straightened away from the desk that she had been leaning against and folded her arms. "You and Liz were made for each other, Quent. Besides, you can't say you're unhappy with the way things turned out."

Quentin cocked his head and leaned back in his chair. "So that was different because you had my best interests at heart, is that it?"

Connor nodded at Allison, then looked back at Quent. "Obviously, unlike Allison here, who had your best interests at heart, Quent, you're just a dirty, rotten interloper of the first order."

* * *

Allison sighed in exasperation. Her brother and Connor were cut from the same cloth, despite the fact that one had been born to wealth and the other still had the air of a dangerous bad boy from the wrong side of the tracks. Neither would back down in a situation like this.

Connor looked at her levelly. "Somehow I didn't think you'd be backing down easily despite seeming docile as a lamb when I drove you to work this morning."

"You do know me better than that," she tossed back.

"Let's call this one a draw, petunia." He said it calmly, but his fixed look conveyed the message that he would not be thwarted next time.

"Why don't you join us for lunch?" Quentin offered. "Connor and I agreed to do lunch today a long time ago, but, as it happens, you've been the number-one topic so far."

She glanced at her watch. "Thanks for the offer but I need to get back."

She'd succeeded in communicating her displeasure to her brother, but it was clear that neither he nor Connor was going to be moved to seeing her point of view—such as the need for Connor to remove himself from her house.

Since staying any longer would probably be an exercise in futility, she supposed that it made sense to agree to Connor's offer of a draw and retreat from the field of battle. But if Connor thought he'd won, he was in for a big surprise.

Connor moved toward her. "I'll go with you."

"You're having lunch with Quent, remember? Besides, it's broad daylight with plenty of traffic."

"Quentin and I can have lunch another time," Connor shot back. "Besides, we've said all we needed to say. My guys are starting on the security system for the house this afternoon and I need to get back." He nodded at Quentin. "You don't mind if I take a rain check, do you?"

Quentin looked quizzically from one to the other of them before, she could swear, a smile played at the corners of his lips. "Not a problem. Not a problem at all."

Her brother's expression made her wary, but she didn't dwell on it as Connor came toward her, obviously intent on following her out the door. "Suit yourselves."

"I'll pick you up at work when you're done," Connor said in a tone that declared he would brook no argument. "Give me a ring on my cell."

"Naturally," she responded sarcastically, though silently she admitted that she'd unintentionally summarized part of the problem: she was afraid that having Connor around might seem all too natural all too quickly.

* * *

On Sunday, Allison drove to Carlyle to have brunch with her family. Her brothers and her sister-in-law had all converged at her parents' impressive brick colonial.

Connor came with her, as she knew he would have even if he hadn't gotten a separate invitation from her parents.

He was still camped out at her townhouse, but she hadn't given up hope of dislodging him. Even if Quentin technically still owned the townhouse and Connor could claim to be acting at his request, that didn't mean she was without options. She wasn't prepared yet to take the drastic step of moving out herself, but she could refuse to cooperate with Connor and ignore him as much as possible.

The main topic of conversation during brunch was, of course, her nameless antagonist. In comparison, the fact that she was living with Connor seemingly went over without anyone so much as batting an eye.

Her mother seemed to summarize the general feeling by commenting, "We're so grateful to you, Connor, for providing your security services. It does give me some peace of mind."

Her brother Matt added, "Lots of luck, Connor. And, if I know Allison, you're going to need it."

Connor merely cocked an eyebrow but Quentin and Noah grinned knowingly.

Allison tossed a quelling look at her brothers—a glance that indicated their hilarity was definitely not appreciated.

By the time brunch was over and she joined her sister-in-law Elizabeth in the family room, she was gritting her teeth. If there was anyone who could sympathize with her plight, however, it would be her best friend.

She flopped into a wicker chair facing Liz. "Can you believe it? Grateful? Peace of mind?" She opened her eyes wide in mock disbelief.

Liz, who'd just taken the rocking chair to breast-feed Nicholas, looked up. "I know, I know. But, Ally, really, aren't you the least bit scared by all this?"

"You mean the threats?" Allison shrugged. "Yes, of course. But I can't let fear paralyze me. Otherwise I might as well resign my job tomorrow."

Liz nodded understandingly.

"But don't tell my brothers that." She blew a breath. "If they knew I was the least bit bothered by this, they'd probably hide me in a hut somewhere with bodyguards posted at all sides."

Liz chuckled. "Oh, Allison, they mean well. Quentin, for one, is genuinely concerned about your safety."

"I know. I just wish they'd give me a little more credit. Besides, there are practically four of them.

Connor could give the other three a run for the money in the overprotectiveness category."

Liz gave her a sympathetic look.

Allison sighed in exasperation. "Connor's made himself at home in the townhouse. Yesterday he was inspecting door locks and checking windows. He already has his people installing a home alarm system with a direct alert to the police."

The alarm system *had* made her more comfortable, she conceded. It was just who was supervising the installation that bothered her.

"Hmm." Liz looked down at the nursing baby. "There was a time when you would have done somersaults for attention from Connor."

Allison made a noncommittal sound in her throat. Liz knew all about her teenaged humiliation at Connor's hands. "I got tired of dining on the crumbs of that table a long time ago."

"I'd be shocked if a daughter of mine were dining on the crumbs of *any* table," Ava Whittaker said as she entered from the doorway leading to the family room.

Allison watched as her mother—looking elegant as always, her coifed hair as dark as Allison's own but tinged with some gray—sank into a nearby wicker chair. "Mom, how could you say that in there?"

"Say what, dear?" Her mother bestowed an indulgent gaze on the baby.

Allison waved a hand. "*Grateful*, Mom? *Peace of*

mind? Whatever happened to 'a woman is perfectly capable of taking care of herself'? Usually I can count on *you* at least in this family."

Her mother had practically raised her children alone while her father built Whittaker Enterprises. When the youngest of her children had reached her teens, Ava had gone to law school and eventually become a respected family court judge. Allison's mother was her hero, her role model.

Her mother's gaze drifted back from the baby to her. "Of course I know you can take care of yourself. But there's nothing wrong with thanking Connor for his help when you may be in real danger." She paused. "In fact, I hope you haven't forgotten the manners I tried to instill in you and have already thanked him yourself. Have you?"

Allison quashed the niggle of guilt. Her mother had a sneaky way of turning the tables on her. "The way all of you were falling over yourselves to thank him, you'd think he'd taken on his worst client ever."

Her mother raised her eyebrows and smiled. "Allison, you know we meant nothing of the kind. Your brothers were just teasing, and usually you're besting them at their own game."

"Yes, well, think of the inconveniences that Connor has to put up with!" Allison sat up in her chair and pretended to think for a second before snapping her fingers. "I know! I made him pace downstairs waiting for me to get ready this morning." She glanced at Elizabeth, who was looking mildly amused. "You know how I *love* long, hot showers."

Her mother tried and failed to look as if she were seriously concerned.

Allison glanced from her mother to Liz and back. "Hasn't it occurred to anyone in this family that I'm, for all intents and purposes, *living with a man?*" She covered her mouth in a mock gasp, then threw up her hands. "I mean, if it had been anyone but Connor, your reaction would have been the opposite of peace of mind and, guaranteed, Matt and Noah wouldn't have been wishing him luck."

"But it *is* Connor, dear." Ava paused. "Unless you're suggesting something *is* going on between the two of you?"

"Of course not!" The thought was ridiculous. "The Kiss" didn't count. "I was just arguing the what if? Is it so beyond the realm of possibility that Connor and I would find living together—" she searched for the right words, then gave up "—sexually awkward?" Not only that, it was too intimate, too personal, too everything!

A gleam came into her mother's eyes. "Oh, I see."

She knew that gleam. The last time her mother had it, she'd just found out Liz and Quentin were having a baby.

Frustrated, Allison slumped back into her chair in defeat. "No, you don't see, Mom."

She'd meant to use the co-habitation issue as a hook to gain some maternal support by making it clear why Connor living with her in the townhouse was an untenable situation. Unfortunately, the plan had backfired: her mother was looking pleasantly surprised.

"Well, what I do understand," Ava said, "is that there's a perfectly nice young man in there."

Allison stared moodily out at the lawn and wondered idly how Connor would have liked being called "a nice young man."

"And, if *someone* were interested, I'd say she couldn't do better."

Allison nodded at Liz. "Can you see her counting the grandbabies? You and Quentin have opened the floodgates."

Liz righted the baby, who'd finished feeding. "Well, you have to admit, Connor is a catch." She added, at Allison's look, "If you were interested, I mean."

"Speaking of grandbabies—" Ava took Nicholas from Liz and placed him over her shoulder to burp. "As much as I love this little sweetheart, my only regret is that Quentin and Liz didn't have time to plan a formal wedding." Ava stood up and started pacing, looking at Allison over the baby's head. "So, my darling, I suggest you make sure to take those long, hot showers by yourself. Leave the cold ones to Connor."

"Mom!"

Liz looked momentarily shocked and then started giggling.

Ava headed to the doorway, a smile on her face.

"We don't even like each other!" Allison called to her mother's retreating back. "We mix like oil and vinegar!"

She turned back to Liz. "Why am I explaining myself?"

"I think you're protesting too much."

She grabbed a pillow from a nearby chair and tossed it at Elizabeth, who laughed and ducked.

The next week was a blur for Allison. Connor had finished seeing to the security system installation at the townhouse, and she and Connor had settled into a regular routine. Each morning, no matter how early, she made it to the front door only to discover Connor was already waiting for her, car keys in hand. If she didn't call him at the end of the day, he'd phone her and ask when he needed to pick her up at the office.

She tried to dodge him on Wednesday, but he just showed up at her office anyway and waited a half-hour for her to finish working. She'd felt like a heel, no matter how much she told herself he deserved it for barging into her life and her house.

Yet, despite doing her best to treat him as if he were no more than a speck of dust on the wall, the two of them continued to rub up against each other. His papers and computer were set up in a corner of her study and his personal belongings were in her house.

But what really bothered her, she admitted to herself, was the intimacy of their living situation. She'd been trying to make a point to her mother when she'd used the words *sexually awkward,* but the truth wasn't far afield.

On Thursday morning, as she was getting ready for work, she'd realized the shirt for the outfit she was putting on was hanging in the hall closet. Knowing Connor was showering, she'd dashed out of her bedroom clad only in her bra and skirt.

She'd just turned to head back to her bedroom, pleased to have found the shirt she'd sought, when the bathroom door had unexpectedly opened and her gaze had collided with Connor's.

His only covering was a towel riding low on his hips. Half-naked, he paradoxically loomed even bigger and more imposing than he usually did.

Her gaze moved downward, taking in lean but sculpted muscles and a line of hair that traveled down a flat stomach and disappeared from view at the top of his towel.

When her gaze connected with his again, she felt herself flush. But whether it was from embarrassment at being caught in her curiosity, or from his hot look at her nearly topless state, or both, she wasn't sure.

She'd involuntarily hugged the shirt to her breast

in a protective gesture and marched past him, slamming her bedroom door shut behind her without turning around.

By Friday night, when Connor had picked her up at work and brought her back to the townhouse, the tension between them was so thick, she felt like a boiling pot with a shaking lid.

After changing out of her business suit and into some jeans and a fitted top, she headed downstairs to fix something simple for dinner and then curl up on the couch to go through some files she'd brought home with her from the office.

Unfortunately, Connor was downstairs in the front hall when she got there. He was loosening his tie and obviously headed upstairs to change out of the business suit he still wore. Somehow he managed to look rough around the edges even in conservative business attire.

He stopped when he saw her and his gaze raked over her, settling on the files she was holding. "What? No plans on a Friday night?"

She stiffened and her chin came up. "I have work to do." Then she added, even though she knew it was ridiculous to feel defensive, "Otherwise I'd have had plans."

"Since when does work mean giving up Friday nights?"

"Sometimes it does." She shrugged. "Besides, I'm

not in the mood to head out tonight." That was partly true. She also wasn't involved with anyone at the moment.

Normally, she'd be heading out anyway, but—and she'd rather eat chalk than admit this to Connor—the truth was that the death threats had nibbled at her self-confidence. So, spending Friday night cocooned at home—even with someone as annoying as Connor—was more appealing than hitting the social scene.

He arched a brow. "Maybe you'd feel differently about staying home if the guys you dated were more interesting."

Her chin came up. "Back off, Rafferty." As if he knew much more about her love life these days than what could be gleaned from the occasional mention about her in the society pages. She set her files down on the console table in the entry hall, where she could find them later.

He looked displeased. "You know what your problem is, petunia?"

She affected a bored tone. "I'm sure you're going to tell me."

"Damn straight, I'm going to tell you. Your problem is you can't deal with a guy who has a brain in his head."

"Don't be ridiculous."

"I've watched you, princess. I've seen all the Tom,

Dick, and Harrys that have gone trooping in and out of your life."

She tossed her hair over her shoulder. "I've never dated a Tom, a Dick—that's with a capital *D*—or a Harry."

Connor's lips twisted. "Of course, I knew I didn't have a chance unless I surgically removed a large segment of my brain."

She wrinkled her nose. "That's a lovely image. Anyway, it's not true. The guys I date are not dumb."

"What about the guy who accidentally bonded his fingers together with glue?"

She sighed impatiently. "Why does everyone bring up Lenny? That was high school and I still can't live that one down."

"In your book, the guys have to look and talk tough but be as thick as a plank," Connor persisted. "Your problem is you've never dated a real man."

"Like you, you mean?"

He smiled slowly, wolfishly. "I haven't heard any complaints."

"You wouldn't. That criticism-proof room your ego dwells in doesn't let you hear any."

His eyes narrowed. "Maybe there aren't any to be heard. I didn't hear any complaints from you about our kiss. In fact, you seemed to enjoy it."

She flushed. "I've had better."

His lips curved into a humorless smile, his jaw

hardening. He moved closer. "Really?" he asked, his voice low and silky.

She lifted her chin up another notch. "Yes, *really*. And, for the record: I didn't enjoy that kiss."

"Hmm." He reached out and clasped her arms with his hands, drawing her closer, his hands moving up and down in a slow caress. "Are you sure?" he murmured.

"Quite."

"Because I could have sworn you were enjoying it."

"Then you were wrong." Was that breathy voice hers?

His gaze dropped to her mouth and he murmured, "Then I must have been imagining those soft lips moving underneath mine."

He thought her lips were soft?

He bent his head and drew in a breath, turning his head to whisper in her ear, "And dreaming that subtle scent of pure woman."

Her body heated.

He drew her flush up against him, his head bending to nuzzle her neck. "I must have fantasized that soft body pressed up against me...."

She should be stepping back—reminding him of the promise she'd extracted about no more kissing—but his low voice and the soothing caress of his hands were having an odd effect on her.

"Admit it," he said softly against her temple. "You

liked the kiss." His hands continued to stroke her, coax her.

It was hard to issue a denial…and hard to remember why it was so important that she do so. His hands moved up to knead her shoulder blades and her eyes nearly closed.

She could feel the magnetism practically radiating from him. He lifted his head and his gaze connected with hers. His eyes shone with a golden-brownish hue in this light. She felt prickles of awareness all over her skin, her nipples tight beneath the concealing fabric of her bra.

"You find me irresistible, don't you, petunia?" he said in a low, seductive voice. "I'm an arrogant, heavy-handed monster, but you like it."

Yes. She should say it out loud and put an end to this. She focused on his mouth. If she said yes, he'd probably kiss her again. She bent toward him—

—and he stepped back, his arms dropping to his sides and the twin flames disappearing from his eyes. "Lucky for us then that I can resist you."

It took her a second, but comprehension finally hit and, with it, a cold fury.

He'd been toying with her! Of all the arrogant, smug…

She was tempted to rear back and punch him. He found her very resistible, did he? He'd enjoyed their kiss just as much as she had, the stinker.

And with that thought, she knew how to wipe the smug smile from his lips. She grasped his lapels and yanked him down to her.

In the instant before her eyes closed, she noted the surprise in his eyes followed by—and she knew she wasn't wrong—male interest.

Four

Her response caught him off guard.

But he'd be damned if he didn't take advantage of the opportunity she'd handed him.

Sure, he'd been trying to rile her. Sure, her refusal to admit their first kiss had affected her had challenged him to prove her wrong. But, the tension that had been building between them all week could almost be cut with the proverbial knife.

So, when one of her hands moved to grasp his shoulder while the other cupped the back of his head, he let her urge him forward and press herself into him as she slanted her mouth across his to deepen their kiss.

Her lips, he thought, were just as soft as he remembered. Enticing. And warm. Definitely warm as they moved over his, caressing, coaxing, rubbing.

He parted his lips and let her take the kiss deeper. His body tightened in instinctive reaction to her nearness.

No matter how much she denied it, the sexual attraction was almost palpable between them. So much so that there was a fine line between their constant baiting of one another and jumping into bed together.

He wrapped his arms around her, lifted her off her feet, and tilted his head back so her mouth was on top of his and she was pressed against him.

She made a sound and started to push away from him, but he tightened his arms around her and took her mouth again and again in a series of increasingly hot kisses that had his blood pounding through his veins.

Finally, when the urge to undress her and take her right there in the entryway started to overwhelm his common sense, he took two strides and had her up against the wall. He lowered her slowly, letting her slide down against him, from her breasts yielding against his chest to her thigh sliding against his arousal.

When her feet had reached the floor, he let her break their kiss.

She blinked and took deep breaths that seemed to mirror his own.

"Want to go another round, petunia?" His voice

sounded husky with arousal to his own ears. "I dare you."

He watched as her brows snapped together and her eyes flashed. It was worth the price of admission to spark her ire, he thought. She'd light into him now all right, but he'd gotten her to convert her outrage into sexual energy twice now, and both times he'd been putty in her hands.

"I don't need another round, Rafferty." Her lashes lowered and her hand came up to stroke his arousal. She looked back up at him, her lips curving seductively. "I have all the proof I need that—how did you put it?—you can resist me."

He sucked in a breath. In an instant, he had her pressed up against the wall again, hands over her head and wrists cuffed by one of his hands.

She wiggled against him, her seductive smile still in place, and he muttered a curse.

"What's that, Connor? I didn't hear you."

He narrowed his eyes. They were playing a dangerous game: both of them refusing to back away from calling the other's bluff. Yet, he was far from being the type to back away from a challenge. "Careful, princess. You might want to think twice about issuing a challenge like that when you've literally got your back to the wall," he growled. "Do you want to deny again you enjoyed our lip-locks? Because, if you do, I'll have to try to prove you wrong *again*."

To her credit, her bravado didn't desert her. She tossed her head, silky strands of dark hair sliding against them both as she tried to clear her face. "I suppose this counts as seduction to a caveman like you."

He tucked a strand of hair behind her ear with his free hand. But then, instead of drawing his hand away, he gave in to temptation and slowly caressed the delicate line of her jaw, letting his thumb rub over the puffy softness of her lower lip.

She held herself still, her gaze locked on his, not yielding, but not lashing him with her sharp tongue either.

He moved his hand downward, stroking the side of her neck and then trailing the tip of his index finger down along the V-shaped neckline of her top and lower, over the roundness of her breast.

With his fingertip, he traced the shape of her breast, moving over its jutting peak.

Allison moaned.

"Watch me," he breathed. He cupped her breast then—noting she was just large enough to fill the palm of his hand—and began to knead her softness.

Her eyes were fixed on his hand, the quickness of her breath the only sign she wasn't immune to his caress.

His pulse came hard and heavy. "It wouldn't take much for us to hit the sack together, petunia."

She looked up at him, her eyes dilated and dark with arousal.

"'Course," he added wryly, "your brothers would probably pound me into pulp if we did. And I wouldn't blame them."

"It wouldn't be any of their business," she said, the breathless quality of her voice belying the toughness of her words.

He found it interesting she didn't immediately deny any interest in sleeping with him. "Right. Ever the independent one, aren't you?"

"It would be nice if you could remember that, too," she said, her words sharp, but, again, her voice carrying that undertone of sexual excitement that was starting to drive him crazy.

"Have you ever wondered what it would be like, petunia," he murmured, "if we took out our frustration with each other in the sack instead of aiming verbal barbs at each other?"

Her eyes widened a fraction but then her brows snapped together. Wrenching her hands free of his grip, she gave him a push. When he took an involuntary step back, she brushed past him, only to turn back, arms folded, when she was free and clear.

She looked furious. *"Have I ever wondered?* Is that an invitation to your bed?"

"If it was, would you accept?"

"Not on your life, Rafferty."

He didn't know what had caused her abrupt change of mood, but he silently cursed himself for inadvertently setting it off.

She marched off in the direction of the living room. "Find some other entertainment for the evening."

The next morning, Allison was feeling marginally more relaxed.

Any remnants of tension from last night she decided to work off at the gym. Connor came along, of course, and bench-pressed some iron while she hit the treadmill.

So much for her aim of ignoring him. *That* plan had fallen by the wayside last night. It didn't help that, despite her best intentions, her eyes kept trailing to him, finding him behind her with the help of the mirror in front of her.

He was in superb physical condition. His biceps and chest muscles flexed as he lifted the weight above his head, held it, and lowered it again, unaware of her scrutiny.

She thought about those arms around her the night before and flushed. Then her mind went back to his words. *Had she ever wondered about hopping into bed with him?*

The question had been like a dousing with ice-cold water, yanking her from the romantic haze she'd fallen into.

Of course, there'd been a time when she'd wondered what it would be like to spend the night with Connor. But his question not only made clear that he hadn't reciprocated her feelings, it had also shown how little he'd known her.

And, naturally, she also couldn't forget that he'd long ago proven himself an insensitive lout.

Another quick look in the mirror revealed Connor was attracting more than his fair share of surreptitious female attention.

Scowling, she ran harder.

Minutes later, she stepped off the treadmill and walked over to where he was now standing by the leg press machine. "I'm going for a swim in the pool."

He gave her a crooked grin. A thin sheen of sweat coated his arm muscles and neck and his T-shirt was darkened in the center with perspiration. He smelled sweaty and all male. "Need to cool off, princess?"

His double meaning wasn't lost on her. She gave him a level look. "Yes, and I thought a few laps in the pool would be a better approach than dumping water over your head."

His laugh sounded behind her as she moved off in the direction of the women's locker room for a quick duck under the shower nozzle before changing into her swimsuit. Since he'd gotten into this gym—not his usual one—with her guest pass, she doubted he'd be following her down to the pool.

She was wrong.

She'd completed three laps and stopped at the side of the pool when she looked up to find him standing above her. They were alone, she noticed peripherally, the middle-aged woman who had been swimming in a nearby lane just disappearing into the locker room.

She trod water and frowned up at him, cocking her head to the side. "I didn't think I'd see you down here." She nodded at his blue swim trunks. "Where did you get those?" she demanded.

"I always come prepared."

Was that amusement she saw lurking in his eyes? If she wasn't mistaken, he knew she'd been thinking—no, hoping—she'd managed to shake him.

Instead, he was looming above her, muscular legs planted near the side of the pool, his hands braced on his hips, his chest and forearms leanly corded and well defined.

Inwardly, she irritatedly shoved down the feminine urge to yield. Outwardly, she shrugged for his benefit. "Suit yourself," she said, and then took off toward the other end of the pool.

Within a few minutes, however, she became aware of him in the lane beside her. She pushed down her annoyance as he stayed with her down one length of the pool and up the other, matching her stroke for stroke.

She paused at the realization. Was that what he

was? she thought. Her match? Is that why she found him so annoying?

She'd thrown her best at Connor over the years and he'd thrown it right back at her. He didn't let her call the shots like a lot of the men she'd dated. Instead, he was an immovable, solid block of granite and she hadn't even made a dent despite years of trying.

Except, last night he'd wanted her. She imagined that if she hadn't made some flippant comment, if she'd taken his offer seriously, they'd have wound up in bed together.

She tested that thought despite herself. In bed with Connor Rafferty. In bed with her nemesis. In bed with the most detestably annoying and implacable man she knew.

Instinctively, she knew that their sleeping together would not be a tame affair. No, they'd take their contentious relationship into the bedroom and they'd be wild and uninhibited and a match of wills and passions.

She knew he found her at least somewhat attractive these days if their recent kisses were anything to go by. So why not just give in and scratch the itch they were both feeling?

She felt warm despite the coolness of the water. It would be so easy to go to bed with Connor—and so complicated—not least because he was currently living in the same house and sleeping just down the hall.

A part of her—the part that was apt to be flattered

by evidence of her feminine power—was thrilled she'd finally gotten Connor's attention, even if it was over ten years too late. That part of her whispered, why not find out exactly what kind of lover he could be?

Still, Connor was Quentin's closest friend. He was so close to her family that Matt and Noah thought of him as an honorary brother. If she gave in to temptation, she might have to deal with seeing her old lover over a family dinner now and then for the rest of her life.

When she found herself touching the side of the pool again, she decided to stop and pull herself upright. Her gaze immediately connected with Connor's hazel one.

He was big and male and disturbingly close, beads of water clinging to his shoulders above the water line. "Nice swim, petunia. Is this how you keep in shape?"

"I enjoy a good swim now and then." She paused. "Alone."

He smiled. "Glad I've been let in on the secret ritual."

"Lucky me."

She swam away from him then and toward the ladder at the side of the pool. He swam after her and she was acutely aware of him watching her get herself out of the pool, water cascading from her body.

She grabbed a towel while he hauled himself out of the water, too. As she headed toward the locker room, he called after her, "Meet you outside in twenty minutes."

She shot him a baleful look over her shoulder. He was shadowing her in the most literal way possible and it was all extremely disturbing.

An hour later, Connor parked in front of the townhouse and followed Allison to her front door. The black metal mailbox nailed to the brick face of the house was half open and visibly stuffed with catalogs and other mail.

He stepped around her before she could react and pulled out the mail in one swift move.

"Last time I checked," she said, her tone annoyed, "it was a federal offense to interfere with the operation of the mail service."

He smiled and watched her irritation grow. "Then consider it checking and not interfering."

She made a grab for the mail, but he moved his arm up and away from her. "Aren't you going to unlock the door?" he asked placidly.

"Don't patronize me."

"Just add it to my tab. I seem to be running a long one with you."

She gave him a haughty look. "That's funny, because I recall stopping your credit line a long time ago."

"Open the door." He nodded at the lock, then looked around. It was broad daylight, not even noon, but he didn't like standing out here with her. They made an easy target. She hadn't gotten any threats since he'd moved in with her, but he knew better than to let his guard down.

After she unlocked the door, he disengaged the alarm system by pressing a few buttons on the box near the door. Then he took a moment to glance through her mail.

The lingerie catalog gave him a moment's pause as he wondered whether she actually wore stuff similar to the skimpy satin bra and undies on the cover.

Tossing the catalog aside, he stopped at a legal-sized white envelope with no return address. He turned it over and, noticing nothing on the back, slid his finger under the flap to tear it open.

"That's my mail!" Allison stormed back over to him from the table where she'd just set down her gym bag. "And don't tell me that you open your clients' mail, too!"

He blocked her attempt to grab the envelope. "In fact, sometimes I do. When the job calls for it."

He slid the contents from the envelope and his blood ran cold. Allison gasped beside him.

There were three photographs of Allison going about her business. The photos were somewhat grainy, computer-generated reproductions taken from a distance, but nevertheless the subject was unmistakable.

Angling himself away from her, he let his eyes

scan the contents of the plain white sheet of paper that had fallen out with the photos. The three lines of typed text chilled him:

Just so you know Im watchin. I can take you out anytime. If you wanna live, quit your job and go vacation on daddy's money.

Allison made a grab for the material in his hand, but he held up his arm. "What is it?" she demanded.

He debated for a second, but realized he'd have no peace until she found out, as much as he wanted to shield her. He wanted to kill the bastard who was threatening her. Tipping the contents of the envelope toward her, he said, "Take a look."

He watched her face blanch and cursed under his breath. "Don't touch anything. I'm calling the police and having them test all the contents of the envelope for fingerprints."

She nodded, uncharacteristically silent.

"Do you recognize when the photos were taken?"

"Two or three weeks ago, I think." She looked up at him and her expression conveyed thinly veiled distress. "That first shot was taken in front of the dry cleaners. My car is over on the far left, which is where I think I parked it when I couldn't find a closer spot. It looks as if the photo was taken from the parking lot across the street."

"Okay, and do you recognize the two others?"

"I think so. I'm wearing something different, but I think those were taken days apart."

He nodded and carefully set down the offending images and sheet of paper. "Good. That'll give the police a good lead about where to start asking questions to see if anyone remembers anything, though I doubt anyone will."

She raked a hand through her hair, the glossy locks cascading around her face. "This is ridiculous. I'm used to having my photo taken from time to time, but it's always been reporters flashing bulbs in my face at a press conference or at a charity ball."

He raised an eyebrow. "Quite the popular little heiress prosecutor, aren't we?"

"Kiss my millionaire fanny, Rafferty."

He laughed, but he privately admitted the joke was on him: he'd certainly given more than a passing thought to kissing her all over.

But, he was glad to see his comment had had its intended effect and there was some fire back in her eyes. That white-faced expression she'd been wearing was unlike her. And while he wanted her to appreciate the danger she could be in, he also didn't want this crazy nut to cow her and mark her for life.

She frowned. "His English skills aren't very good, are they?"

"Yeah, which does point to our man Taylor or,

more precisely, one of his gang members who isn't behind bars."

"Hmm. Maybe." She looked unconvinced. "Or it could just be someone trying to throw us off the scent and point the finger elsewhere."

"What makes you think that?" He had his own theory in that regard, but he was interested in hearing hers.

She crossed her arms. "If one of Taylor's pals wanted me dead, I'd probably already be gone—or, at least, they wouldn't have bothered with a note."

He nodded. She'd obviously learned a few things at the DA's Office. He just wasn't sure he liked her being acquainted with the seedier side of life. Sure, he'd often made fun of her diamond-studded-slipper upbringing, but he knew better than most just how bad the alternative could be.

"The person who is doing this obviously wants to scare me," Allison mused, "but so far he's hung back from doing more than threaten. So, again, we have a profile that might fit better with Kendall, who's a white-collar criminal."

"You know something, petunia?"

"What?" Her chin came up, as if expecting a sarcastic remark.

"You took the words right out of my mouth."

Her shoulders relaxed a little. "That's probably the highest compliment in your book."

Five

Allison didn't know why she'd let Connor talk her into spending the weekend at his getaway cottage in the Berkshires, west of Boston. Somehow she'd let him convince her that she needed the change of scene.

She sat in the living room, her files around her, having spent the afternoon working on her brief in response to Kendall's attorney's pre-trial motion to exclude certain evidence from being presented to the jury.

She could hear Connor moving around in the kitchen. After they'd gone into town for groceries, he'd gone to work on his computer. There were four of them in the den, she had discovered, plus some hi-tech computer accessories.

She was thankful that the past week had been less eventful than last Saturday. After they'd discovered the anonymous note in her mailbox, the rest of the day had been spent talking to the police that Connor had summoned to the townhouse. She'd spent more than an hour being grilled, the dull throbbing at her temples a testimony to the thoroughness of their questioning.

The police had since informed them that the photographs and note hadn't turned up any fingerprints other than Connor's, though the envelope that they had come in had had many different prints, including probably that of her mailman. None of the shop owners or anyone else near the locations where the photographs had been taken had remembered anything suspicious.

Yet, despite the uneventfulness of the week, she hadn't felt relaxed. Whereas before she'd only thought someone might be watching her, the photographs confirmed that to be the case.

It was a spooky and unsettlingly thought. She now found herself turning around at odd moments, expecting to catch someone watching her.

So, at the end of the week, when Connor had argued she could work just as well at his country house as she could at the townhouse, she hadn't disagreed too strenuously. In fact, she admitted to herself, having him around made her feel safe. Perhaps it was the photos and note that had done it, but she no longer had the same desire to get rid of him.

And going to Connor's place *was* a distraction. When they'd arrived that morning, she'd discovered that Connor's "getaway cottage" was a two-story, wood-frame structure nestled in the woods, well back from the road. It boasted four bedrooms, two baths, a spacious kitchen, a living room, dining room, den, deck and, for good measure, a hot tub.

She tried hard not to think about the hot tub—and tried harder still not to think about the fact that her bedroom was next to his.

She looked through the sliding-glass doors leading to the outdoor wooden deck and watched Connor fire up the barbecue grill. Beside him, plates held some steaks and potatoes, ready for grilling.

Deciding it was time to put away her files for the evening, she rose and gathered up her papers, putting them in a neat stack on an end table.

When she got outside, Connor was nursing a beer and watching the rays of the disappearing sun twinkle through the branches of the trees.

He opened another beer and handed it to her.

"Thanks," she said, watching as he expertly used a long fork to turn the steaks. "You know, I could almost get used to having you cook for me, Rafferty."

At his astonished look, she laughed. "But I suppose grilling is up there with manly pursuits like knowing how to open a beer bottle and programming a remote control."

Seemingly despite himself, he chuckled. Closing the barbecue, he said, "You got that right, petunia. So for the rest of the evening, remember that I'm the one in charge and you're the deputy."

She rolled her eyes. "What do you mean for the rest of the evening? That's what you try to convince me of every day."

"Right, but with little success." He nodded through the glass doors at the kitchen. "The rest of the stuff for dinner is in there."

Tossing him a look, she nevertheless took the hint and went to the kitchen. She returned with plates, utensils, and napkins for the outdoor table. She also carried out the salad he'd left on the kitchen counter.

As she set the table, she cast him a surreptitious look. His faded jeans did little to hide a tight rear end. He wore his button-down plaid shirt open at the collar, where it revealed a small bit of the white undershirt he wore beneath. Overall, the effect was casual but sexy.

Until they'd actually sat down to eat, Allison didn't realize how intimate it was to be having dinner alone with Connor, surrounded by the woods, eating food that he'd prepared. Despite that—or maybe as a distraction from it—the conversation flowed easily between them. They talked about the latest news, what the Boston Red Sox could do to make it to the World Series, and what qualified as classic rock-and-roll music.

As a result, by the time they were done eating, she was feeling pleasantly relaxed. So much so that she was able to say casually, "There's one thing I never understood about you, Rafferty."

"Only one?" He quirked a brow and sat back, looking amused. "What a letdown. I don't even qualify as complex, misunderstood, or—better yet—tortured?"

She rolled her eyes. "James Dean was tortured, you're just—" she paused to think for a few seconds "—inscrutable."

"Inscrutable?" He rubbed his chin. "Okay, I guess that's better than nothing. So, I suppose you're going to enlighten me about what makes me 'inscrutable'?"

Ignoring his mocking tone, she plunged ahead. "As I was saying, there's one major thing I haven't understood about you." She took a fortifying sip of her beer. "It's this whole South Boston business."

His expression, she noted, became ever so slightly shuttered.

Nevertheless, because she wasn't one to turn back once she'd started, she went on, "You leave South Boston, get a fancy degree from Harvard—with high honors in computer science, no less—and then, instead of starting the corporate climb at some cushy investment banking job, you wind up going back to South Boston to set up shop."

He shrugged.

"Not only that," she persisted, "but you choose an unglamorous area like security systems. Most people don't go to Harvard just to come full circle."

He sat back in his chair and studied her. "True, but things worked out well anyway." He nodded around him to the large house and the surrounding trees. "Maybe, princess, it was all part of the master plan."

She nodded. "Knowing you, I don't doubt it. What I want to know is, what was the master plan?"

He looked amused. "You just keep probing until you get some answers, don't you? Which is probably what makes you a great prosecutor."

"Don't try to sidetrack me with compliments." She steeled herself against his flattery and leaned forward in her seat. "Why go back to South Boston after Harvard? One would assume you had every reason not to, particularly since your father was killed in the line of duty there."

She knew from Quentin that Connor's father had been a cop who had died when Connor was still a kid. She also knew Connor's mother, a nurse, had died of breast cancer soon after his high-school graduation, leaving him parentless from the age of eighteen. It had all made her feel very sorry for Connor when she'd met him.

"Am I being cross-examined?" Connor's tone was casual, but she sensed an underlying tenseness in him.

Knowing that she was on to something, she ignored his question and said, instead, "Tell me about your father." She added, gentling her voice, "Please. I'd really like to know."

He saluted her with his empty beer bottle. "Okay, princess, I see I'm not going to throw you off."

She wondered if that were true. She got the feeling he was only going to give her an answer because he wanted to—and she also sensed she was on terrain that Connor didn't ordinarily let people onto.

He was silent for a time, looking off into the distance before his gaze came back to her. "I was nine when Dad died. Tough age to lose your father—but no age is a good one. He was the assistant coach of my softball team and taught me the usual stuff: how to ride a bike, how to swim."

He blew a breath, then continued, "My father had this thing about giving back to the community. Perhaps because he'd grown up as a working-class kid in South Boston himself and had gone on to become a cop."

"Hmm," was all she said. She'd finally gotten him going and she wasn't going to give him the opportunity to get sidetracked by her commentary.

"Anyway, even though we could have afforded to live out in the suburbs, he wanted to stay in South Boston. He even angled his way to a job there."

"In other words, he was into 'community policing' even before the term was coined," she put in.

He nodded. "Exactly. He believed not only in police patrols, but police involvement in the community."

"Getting to know people," she supplied. "Coaching softball as a way to keep kids off the streets."

He nodded again. "Right."

She waited for him to go on.

He took a swig of his beer, then squinted into the distance as if he was trying to make out something among the trees. "One day the doorbell rang and I thought it was him, back from the evening shift. Instead it was the sergeant from his district, looking so serious I immediately got a queasy feeling in my stomach." He shifted his gaze back to hers. "You can guess what came next."

"How did it happen?" she asked softly. They'd known each other for years but this was the first time she'd felt comfortable enough to ask him about the circumstances of his father's death. She ached for the boy who had opened the door to a nightmare so many years ago.

"He was responding to a break-and-enter. He caught one guy, cuffed him. What he didn't know was the guy had a partner who was packing a .38 special."

Allison flinched at the image he evoked.

Connor grinned crookedly. "You wanted to know, princess."

"What I want to know is why you bury that story."

"Ever combative and feisty, aren't you?"

She frowned. "Maybe, but there's certainly nothing to be ashamed of in that story. I have no idea why you keep quiet about it. In fact—"

"In fact," he finished for her, "people might have felt sorry for me and gone out of their way to help, is that what you were going to say?"

"Well, yes—"

"And that's exactly what I didn't want," he said, his look almost combative. "That's exactly how the people who did know—at my father's precinct and in the neighborhood—did act." His brows drew together. "I didn't need their sympathy. It wasn't going to bring my father back. And I sure as hell didn't want anyone thinking I was trading on a tragedy."

His words were startling. And, yet, they were in keeping with what she knew him to be: proud, tough, private.

"Curiosity satisfied, petunia?" he asked, rising with his empty plate. His tone wasn't mocking, just matter-of-fact.

"Thank you for telling me," she said simply, picking up her own plate and utensils and following him inside, where she deposited her load in the sink. "I can't even imagine how hard it was for you and your mother."

He leaned back against the kitchen counter, legs casually crossed at his feet. "Yeah, it was devastating for Mom. She went back into nursing to earn some money, but South Boston was all she knew, so that's where we stayed."

"You must have been lonely."

"No," he said, shaking his head. "I was a terror. My father had been killed and I was mad as hell at the world. I fought, I skipped school and I took unnecessary risks. What finally turned me around was a combination of my mother and some well-meaning high-school teachers meting out tough love, and my own realization that I had a brain and I might as well use it in a way that got me somewhere."

She went to perch on a bar stool. "Which brings me back to my original question. Why go back to South Boston after all that? You could have gone anywhere after Harvard, and you had every reason to."

"Like I said, you're tenacious." He gave her a once-over with his eyes, then smiled at her scowl. "When I started my business, I was looking to keep overhead low. The neighborhood is changing, but the rent on a rinky-dink apartment in South Boston at the time was the right price. It was as simple as that."

She nodded. Suddenly, turning down a cushy big law firm job for the DA's Office while living in a

ANNA DePALO   87

townhouse in exclusive Beacon Hill didn't seem
like much of a sacrifice. "Every time I come across
a profile of you in the newspapers or in magazines,
they always mention that you headed back to South
Boston to start your business."

He quirked a brow. "You read all the bios of me,
princess?"

She felt herself grow red. "Just when the only alternative is reading the instructions on medicine
bottles."

He grinned. "You don't give an inch do you?"

"You don't either," she retorted. "Anyway," she
said, going back to the subject at hand, "Rafferty
Security still has an office in South Boston,
doesn't it?"

"Yeah, you could say that…."

His hesitancy puzzled her. She knew her information wasn't wrong and the question had almost been
rhetorical. "Well, what else would you say?"

He coughed, then folded his arms.

"Yeees?" she prompted. If she didn't know better,
she'd say he looked uncomfortable.

"It's not really an office. It's more like a commu-
nity-relations clearinghouse."

She frowned for a second, then laughed. "You
mean you operate a charity there?"

He shifted. "That's about right."

The urge to tease was irresistible. "Don't tell me

the oh-so-tough Connor Rafferty has a soft spot. Or should I just call you Connor P.—for philanthropist—Rafferty?"

"We don't call them philanthropists in South Boston, petunia."

She cocked her head. "Oh, really? What do you call them, then? Benefactors? Charitable donors? People so rich they give their money away?" She was so enjoying this. "Face it, Connor, you're just like those well-heeled do-gooders you dislike. You know," she said, throwing his words back at him, "like those debutantes who organize charity auctions."

He acknowledged her teasing with a raised eyebrow but then shook his head. "I wasn't born rich. There's a difference."

Rather than argue with him, she asked, "What does this charitable organization do? And, by the way—" she held up a hand "—while I'm enjoying this enormously because I like tweaking your nose about your closet philanthropy, I'm delighted you've seen fit to try to do good in the world."

"This 'charitable organization,' as you put it, sponsors programs for neighborhood kids."

"Very good." She nodded. "I'm just surprised you're not doing something more tied to Rafferty Security's line of business."

He looked surprised for a second.

"What?"

"We are. Good guess." He added, "We offer self-defense classes and classes on home security."

"Ah," she said.

"I can see that light bulb going on in your head."

"Well, it does explain a lot after all. Your father was into giving back to the community and you grow up and move back to South Boston and set up a charity. Not only that, but your father died thwarting a burglary and you go into the security business."

He shoved away from the kitchen counter. "Connecting those dots is easy, petunia. Just don't read too much into it. I don't."

"Why? Are you saying your father's death had nothing to do with it?" she persisted.

"What I'm saying is you ask too many questions," he grumbled. "But, yeah, I'll concede the influence."

Despite his casual tone, she knew she'd finally penetrated a bit below the facade that Connor Rafferty presented to the world. She'd also gained some insight into the source of Connor's protective instincts.

She really should give him some slack, she thought, even though she disliked the way he had come barging into her life. Having suffered one tragic loss, he was obviously protective of those close to him—and that protective instinct even extended to helping his former neighbors.

"What are you thinking, princess?" he asked. "I can almost see the wheels turning in that head of yours."

She gave her head a slight shake, her lips curving upward. "It's hard to believe, but I was feeling almost inclined to like you."

He stared at her intensely for a moment, then said, "You should smile more often."

Their eyes caught and held before she looked away, feeling suddenly uncharacteristically shy and awkward.

"What about you, petunia?" he said, leaning back against the kitchen counter and breaking the mood. "Your mother is a judge and you're a prosecutor. Seems to me you're just as guilty of some semi-conscious influences."

She relaxed as they seemed to be back on safer ground. "Psychoanalyze away," she said lightly, "but you should know the analogy doesn't work well. If I'd really wanted to make my family happy, I'd have stayed away from prosecuting criminals at the DA's Office and gone to some nice, comfy law-firm job." She wrinkled her nose. "You know, doing non-profit law or some such, which would have dovetailed nicely with all those charity auctions I'm supposed to be organizing."

He grinned, seeming to recognize the jab at him and his comment the night he'd shown up at her townhouse. "All right," he said, folding his arms, "maybe I was too quick to judge."

She gave him a look of mock skepticism. "You think?"

* * *

Ignoring her bait, Connor realized it was time to turn the tables on her. She'd probed and poked and made him realize and acknowledge more than he'd wanted to. He figured he was entitled to reciprocate. "Why do you do it?"

"Do what?"

"Work at the DA's Office when you clearly don't have to, and when you could have gotten a cushier job, which your family clearly expected you to do."

She cocked her head to the side and contemplated him for a second, as if considering how much to divulge.

"Fess up, princess. You're not the only one who knows how to be dogged with questions." She looked deliciously delectable perched on the bar stool, her long legs encased in snug blue jeans, a cotton top outlining a pert and enticingly rounded chest.

"Would you believe me if I said a passion for justice?" she asked. "Before a late-life career in the law, my mother was the queen of those philanthropic charity benefits you're so fond of. I guess some of that do-gooder stuff rubbed off on me and my brothers."

"And yet, your family wasn't thrilled by your choice of the DA's Office." Connor forced himself to focus on what they were talking about despite the weight that had settled in his groin.

She looked down as if to shield her expression

from him, stretching out her legs as she did so, one of the mules she was wearing dangling from her foot. "You may have noticed they're rather protective."

"No more so than with you, the baby of the family and the only girl," he finished for her.

She looked up, her eyes meeting his. "Exactly."

He smiled. "Well, you sure as heck didn't make it easy on them. From what I recall, you did a good job of rattling the bars of the cage."

She gave him a meaningful look. "You'd know something about that, wouldn't you?"

He held up his hands in mock surrender. "Let's make a deal to steer clear of that episode in the bar. I'll admit it wasn't one of my finer moments. I usually don't deal in trickery."

She looked somewhat mollified by his almost apology, but he couldn't help adding, "Anyway, it's not as if that night in the bar was out of character for you."

"Oh?"

There was a wealth of meaning in that "oh" and, if he knew what was good for him, he should probably shut up now. Unfortunately, he was rarely one to shut up where Allison was concerned. "What about the year you started a campaign to get all the high-school girls to *accidentally on purpose* show up for class braless?" He grinned. "As I recall, it was the first time your school had to make a rule about underwear."

"We were making a political statement!"

"Yeah, to the enjoyment of the male half of the student body," he said dryly. He'd heard about the ensuing ruckus from Quentin.

"The point," she said tightly, "was to show that if one girl wore a top without a bra one day, it was no big deal, but, if every girl went without a bra every day, it would be disruptive. In other words, we could wield a lot of power by joint action. After that, we were able to get some real change through the student council."

"So is that what the DA's Office is all about? Just more of your maverick tendencies?" he asked. "Or were you just trying to make your family crazy?"

"It's debatable whether I drove them crazier than they drove me," she muttered.

"Ah."

"The DA's Office is the first time I felt I had established an identity for myself apart from my family. I wasn't Allison Whittaker, heiress, daughter of philanthropists James and Ava, sister of Quentin the tycoon, Matt the enigma, Noah the playboy."

"I see."

"Do you really?" she asked. "At the DA's Office, I was first and foremost Allison Whittaker, Assistant DA. Many of the defendants in my cases hadn't even heard of the Whittakers. And, the other lawyers at the DA's Office didn't care what my last name was as long as I was pitching in with everyone else to help dig us out from under the mountain of cases."

Her voice had risen half an octave and her words had started coming faster. He'd touched a nerve, that was for sure.

The DA's Office had been a means to independence for Allison and he'd been making light of it. Suddenly he was sorry for that.

"Do you really understand, Connor?" she continued. "Because sometimes you seemed to act no better than my brothers."

"Believe me, the last thing I feel for you is brotherly," he said, half under his breath. Her impassioned speech had brought a spark to her eyes and a boldness to her body language that his libido was intuitively responding to.

"What?" she asked, although the arrested look on her face said she'd heard him.

"Did you not hear me, petunia?" he asked, meeting her eyes directly. "Or is it that you just can't believe what you heard?"

All the reasons he'd given himself over the years not to test the waters with Allison flew out the window. In reality, he had already tested the waters where she was concerned, and, now that he had had a taste of her, the need for more was irresistible.

She gave a laugh that sounded forced. "I imagine it was hard to feel brotherly when I was a thorn in your side."

He pushed back from the counter. "Loss of courage isn't something I'd ever have thought to accuse you of."

They were alone in the woods together at the getaway cottage he'd recently finished building and where he'd brought no other woman. Suddenly, he didn't give a damn about the consequences of getting romantically involved with her. All that mattered was now.

The threat she'd gotten in the mail, the proof that some nut had been watching her, waiting to strike, all that hammered home that he could have lost her already.

He might not have tomorrow—to laugh with her, to make love to her—and he'd be damned if he was going to wonder any longer about what might, could, or should have been.

She straightened on the stool, her brows drawing together. "I don't know what you're talking about."

"Don't you?" he asked softly. With two strides, he was in front of her, within touching distance. To her credit, she stayed where she was, her chin coming up in that way she had when she was getting ready verbally to sock it to him.

He almost smiled as he reached out to touch her.

"Don't," she said on a breath. It wasn't fear in her eyes—or panic—but a turbulent set of emotions.

"Why not?" The urge to touch her was overwhelming and there didn't seem to be a reason in the world not to give in to it. "Because your brothers would beat me to a pulp?" He raised her chin, his thumb caressing her lower lip. "I think I'll risk it," he murmured.

Six

Allison felt prickles of awareness all over her skin at Connor's touch. She knew if they slept together, nothing would be the same again.

This wasn't just about one kiss or one night. This was about getting tangled up with a man who wouldn't be as easy to handle as any of the ones she'd dated in the past. Connor would challenge her, and there'd be no smug assurance that she was in control.

When she still hadn't said anything, the light went out of Connor's eyes and his hand dropped away from her mouth. She hadn't voiced an invitation—and he hadn't read one in her eyes—so he was backing off.

In that instant, however, she knew she couldn't let this moment pass. He offered comfort and safety in a world that had become a much scarier place. And, while she knew she could always stand on her own two feet if she had to, she also knew that now—tonight—she wanted that comfort.

Suddenly, she couldn't wait to dive in to his arms. The possibility that she wouldn't be in control was more of a temptation than a risk to be avoided.

She slid off the stool, bringing them nearly flush up against each other.

His usual cocky facade was not on display. Instead, what she saw was raw hunger and naked desire.

Her breath caught in her throat. "Connor…"

She placed her hands on his chest and felt the strong, rhythmic beat of his heart. He held himself very still as she went up on tiptoe, searched his face, and then, slowly, very slowly, pressed her lips to his.

His mouth opened under the pressure of her lips, his lips rubbing, stroking against hers. He took his time—as if he had all the time in the world—letting her lead, then demanding more. Yet, he held his arms at his sides, his mouth the only part building a response from her.

Yes, she thought, the man definitely knew how to kiss.

Just when she was on the point of making sounds

of frustration, however, he appeased her need and wrapped his arms around her.

The kiss deepened, his tongue slipping between her lips to swirl within her mouth and duel with hers.

She moaned and her fingers threaded through his hair. She couldn't get close enough to him—couldn't get enough of him.

When he finally tore his mouth from hers, he said huskily, "Wrap your legs around me." She readily complied and his hands splayed across her bottom, supporting her weight.

In this position, his erection pressed into the most intimate part of her and, instinctively, she rubbed against him.

He muttered an oath as he headed for the stairs leading to the bedrooms. "Do that again and we won't make it to the bed."

She laughed breathlessly. "What about the couch down here?"

He stopped for a second and gave her a smoldering look. "I want to see you lying in my bed. I want to see your thick, dark hair spread out across my pillow." He leaned forward so his forehead rested against hers, then added, his voice deep, "I want to see you, I want to hear you and, most importantly, I want to taste you while you're lying on my bed."

"Is that an order?" she quipped.

He straightened and started up the stairs, hoisting

her higher and giving her a wry grin. "No, but I hope I've answered your question. There *is* a couch down here, but *we* won't be using it."

"Can you hurry then?" she joked, almost hurting with the wanting. It seemed as if she'd been waiting for this moment forever and now need threatened to sweep her away.

At the end of the hallway upstairs, he kicked open the door to his bedroom and, in two strides, crossed the room to the bed, coming down half on top of her.

There was almost no thought then: need consumed them. They were like two people who had crossed the desert and finally come to a stream of water.

She was dimly aware of kicking off her sandals and of Connor helping her slide her top over her head. Then, with a flick of his fingers, he undid the front clasp of her bra.

"You're perfect," he groaned, his gaze hot on her breasts, which were capped by nipples that were tight and hard and peaked. Under his gaze, they became even more so.

"They're just average breasts," she muttered, embarrassed.

"Perfect," he repeated in a low voice. Then, with his eyes never leaving hers, he slowly lowered his head to one breast. She sighed when his mouth closed around her nipple.

Waves of sensation threatened to take her under as she watched him use his mouth on her.

When he moved his mouth to her other breast, she threaded her fingers through his hair and let her eyes close. A restless longing had taken hold of her, making her limbs quiver and suffusing her with a liquid warmth.

His mouth left her breast and seized her lips and she wound her arms around his neck, meeting his questing mouth kiss for kiss until he finally pulled back with a groan and sat up.

She opened her eyes and nearly moaned in protest until she saw the desire written on his face. Raising herself on her elbows, she watched as he quickly rid himself of his plaid shirt and then yanked his white undershirt over his head.

His chest had only a sprinkling of hair, so there was little to conceal the muscles that defined his chest and upper arms.

She'd seen him shirtless several times over the years, when he'd come to pool parties at the Whittakers', and, memorably, when she'd spied him in the process of removing his sweat-stained shirt and putting on a fresh one during a school-break construction job in Carlyle.

She'd fantasized about touching him then. Now, she sat up to run her hands along the sculpted muscles.

"Yes, touch me," he muttered. "Make me burn, petunia."

She reveled in the power she had to affect him.

She pressed her lips where her hands had been, placing hot, wet kisses over the planes of his chest.

He stopped her only so he could rid them both of their shoes and jeans. He peeled the denim off her in one fluid movement, taking along the underwear underneath.

His hand splayed on her hip as they fell back onto the bed again and their lips met in a deep, hungry kiss.

His hand caressed her leg, then moved to her inner thigh, making her tingle with anticipation.

She tore her mouth from his. "Ah, Connor…"

"Shh," he said as his hand slid up to the juncture of her thighs. Holding her, his eyes steady on hers, his finger parted her and he caressed her inside.

"Oh!"

"Yes," he said in a smoky voice. "Let me hear how it makes you feel, petunia."

She clutched his shoulders, his look of possession the last thing she saw as her eyes closed and her world spiraled beyond everyday sensation in response to the sure and steady rhythm of his hand.

"Connor!" The cry was torn from her as she entered oblivion.

When Allison floated back down to earth, Connor was lying next to her, facing her, his arm bent and his head propped up on his hand. His other hand was drawing lazy circles on her thigh.

She looked down and he followed her gaze.

"Yup, I still want you," he said, a hint of humor lacing his voice.

She looked back up at him. He was looking just a wee bit too pleased with himself, she decided. Giving him a coy look through her lashes, she said, "Well, thanks for everything," and made to rise.

Laughing, he pushed her back onto the bed. "Not so fast, princess. I think we have some unfinished business."

"Really?" She feigned innocence. "And that would be…?"

Instead of responding, he drew her to him, his mouth coming down on hers, and she was lost again in the sea of emotion and sensation between them.

He was the most magnificent man she'd ever been with. Connor's physical size made her feel small and dainty despite her statuesque five-foot-eight frame. His scent—the warm muskiness of all-male—enveloped her.

He kissed her deeply, hungrily, his mouth plundering. She opened her mouth to him even as he parted her legs, making room for himself.

She reached down then and grasped his erection, stroking him until he released her mouth with a growl. "I'm about to come out of my skin, petunia."

"That's what I was hoping for," she teased.

"You don't have to hope anymore," he countered, then smiled so wolfishly he made her giggle.

He opened a drawer in the nightstand and retrieved a small foil packet. Turning back to her, he cleared his throat and said, "Before you jump to conclusions, I'm going to tell you that you're the only woman I've ever brought out here with me."

She opened and shut her mouth.

"And secondly," he went on, "I didn't bring protection along because I was sure of myself. I just thought being prepared wouldn't be a bad idea given the fireworks exploding between us lately."

She felt ridiculously pleased about being the only woman he'd brought to his refuge in the Berkshires. She took the packet from him and, ignoring his surprised and then delighted look, rolled the protection slowly onto him.

"Ah, Allison," he sighed.

She gave him a quick peck on the lips.

He spread her legs then and positioned himself. "Last chance, princess," he said and, despite his lighthearted tone, she knew he was holding himself tightly in check.

In some ways, it seemed she'd been waiting for this moment her whole life. She'd be darned if she'd beat a retreat now—the consequences for tomorrow be damned. She was about to find out if the reality lived up to all her girlhood fantasies.

"Not a hope, Rafferty." She wrapped her legs about him and raised her hips.

He groaned as he slid into her. "Ah, petunia—"

She gasped, then sighed.

He set a rhythm that she took up, meeting him with counterpoint thrusts, the momentum building in tandem with the tension between them until it burst forth and sent her spiraling into a starry darkness, her hands clutching spasmodically on Connor's shoulders and feeling the thin sheen of sweat that had broken out on his skin.

Dimly, she heard him give a hoarse groan and take his own release.

Connor came back to reality slowly. He felt as if he'd been passed through a wringer; he was spent, his muscles weak with release. Paradoxically, he felt gloriously alive.

Before tonight, he'd thought the sexual tension between him and Allison was a strong sign they'd be explosive in bed together.

He hadn't been wrong.

He looked over at Allison. Her eyes were closed, their ebony lashes flickering against her fair skin. A slight smile played at the corners of her lips.

She'd blown him away. If he'd had any clue, he wondered whether he could have resisted her as long as he had, even with the many reasons it made sense to do so.

And that was the problem, he acknowledged. Those reasons had not gone away.

His job was to protect Allison, not bed her. She was still the daughter of the couple who'd treated him as if he were a surrogate son. She was Quentin's baby sister. Someone whom he, along with her brothers, had treated for years as if she were a spoiled brat.

He closed his eyes. He didn't—couldn't—regret what had just happened. It had been the most glorious sexual experience of his life. But what was he supposed to say to Quentin next time he saw him? *I slept with Allison and, hey, it was better than I ever fantasized?*

'Course, then he'd have to let Quentin deck him. He'd been asked to be her bodyguard, not her lover.

And yet, the attraction between him and Allison had been simmering for a long time. The threat against her had simply been the match that had ignited the tinderbox that they'd shoved their attraction into so they could safely ignore it.

He was going to have to tread carefully, that was for sure. Among other things, he had to figure out sooner rather than later who was making the death threats. After that, he could focus on figuring out what uncharted territory he and Allison had steered their relationship into.

He glanced back over at her sleeping face.

Whether Allison was going to admit it or not, what they'd started tonight wasn't finished.

Allison woke to the smell of fresh coffee. Had she set the automatic timer on her coffee pot?

She rolled over and opened her eyes. Dark wood ceiling beams greeted her. She frowned, momentarily disoriented. Where was she?

And then it all came rushing back…the death threat in the mail…her agreement to come out to the Berkshires with Connor despite her better judgment…their intimate dinner…the two of them tangling the sheets together.

She flushed. He'd certainly lived up to her fantasies and then some.

They'd woken up in the middle of the night, and they'd had at each other in a way that had been just a bit less mind-blowing than the first time.

More importantly, she knew that last night she'd seen a side of Connor that he rarely let anyone glimpse. She'd seen vulnerability when he'd talked about his father's death and she'd realized his protective instincts ran deep and strong.

Then he'd made love to her tenderly and passionately.

Made love. Was that literally what it had been?

Her mind shied away from the question.

Certainly he desired her. She hugged the sheet to

her as she thought about Connor's demonstration of desire last night.

She had to admit their relationship had changed irrevocably.

Footsteps sounded on the stairs.

She groaned. Leave it to Connor not to give her a moment to freshen up and look presentable.

"Rise and shine, princess."

He was dressed in a beat-up T-shirt and jeans and his hair still appeared damp from his shower. He looked positively yummy.

A smile played at the corners of his lips. He held out the steaming cup in his hand. "I brought your shot of caffeine. I was going to hold it under your nose to resuscitate you, but I see you're awake."

She sprang up in bed and held out her hands. "Bless you."

He handed her the cup and then sat on the side of the bed. "Cream, no sugar."

She sipped. "Mmm. Excellent. How did you guess?"

He shrugged nonchalantly. "There are a few things I've picked up about you over the years. One of them is how you like your coffee."

"Part of your dossier on me?"

He looked at her enigmatically. "You could say that."

"Hmm." She lowered her eyes and sipped. "Thanks for bringing the coffee. It really wasn't necessary."

She again felt the same uncharacteristic shyness
with him that she'd felt last night, before…before…
As she felt herself start to blush, she yanked her
mind back from that trail of thought.

"Actually, it was necessary," he said matter-of-factly.

She quirked a brow, struggling for the casual, un-
caring attitude that had been so easy to adopt where
he was concerned—before last night.

"I'll admit to a selfish desire to see how you
looked lying in my bed this morning."

She couldn't resist asking, "And how do I look?"

"Like a woman who's been thoroughly made love
to." His eyes were hot. "Just like I imagined."

She felt herself heat. "You're crazy."

He nodded. "Yep, crazy for you. Though I have
to admit jumping your bones last night was a good
antidote for that. At least temporarily."

Oh, boy. Somehow Connor's new sexually tinged
teasing was more dangerous than his old sarcastic tone.

"May need to inoculate myself every day though,"
he mused, making a show of rubbing his chin in
thought. "Strikes me as the kind of thing that wears
off easily."

She nearly choked on her coffee. Every day?

He looked amused as he caught her reaction. "Don't
worry, petunia. If last night was any measure, you're
more than up to the task. I guess it shouldn't have come

as a surprise that we'd be dynamite in bed together, given how we're used to ripping into each other."

"Hmm," she said, shrugging as if he'd just told her nothing more significant than what the weather was outside, "I guess I should be flattered."

He stood up, grinned. "Get dressed before I'm tempted to give you another demonstration of how flattered you should be."

Allison cupped her chin in her hand and stared out at the rain from her kitchen window. She knew she probably had a dreamy, dopey expression on her face but it had been a week since they'd gotten back from the Berkshires and the week had been close to idyllic.

Her relationship with Connor had settled into a better routine, one tinged with tentative exploration. After Connor picked her up at the office, they usually cooked dinner together and then worked or watched a movie. She was pleasantly surprised to discover Connor's skills in the kitchen extended to more than cooking pancakes and grilling.

"Necessity," he'd said with a grin. "Single guy living alone either cooks or goes hungry. After a while, it gets boring eating food straight from a can."

She'd made a face and he'd laughed out loud.

She'd also discovered that their taste in movies differed. He liked action-adventure flicks while she preferred romantic comedies, so they'd settled on legal dramas with a romantic subplot.

Their evenings had usually ended in her candle-lit, floral-scented bedroom with its pointelle-blanket-covered brass bed. It had been amusing to watch Connor invade such a wildly feminine room and she'd laughed as he'd gingerly settled in.

Despite the threats looming over her head, the past week had left her with a feeling of contentment and sense of well-being she'd never experienced before.

She knew she was in danger of falling in love with Connor. Rather than feel alarm, however, she felt joyously happy.

There was no doubt that Connor wanted her. Her face heated as she recalled how many different ways he'd demonstrated that. And—as she'd once told her sister-in-law Elizabeth when she'd thought she'd been having trouble with Quentin—want was often the road to love.

If Connor didn't love her yet, he nevertheless could come to realize he had deeper feelings for her. Especially if the future was anything like the past week.

She glanced up at the late-Saturday sky again. The rain hadn't let up and Connor still hadn't returned from his business meeting. She'd been expecting him an hour ago so they could run some errands, the most important of which was to pick up some more groceries.

She'd been planning all day for a candlelit dinner.

Just the two of them, clinking wineglasses, tasting her pear salad, and then dining on a meal of pheasant with pecan stuffing, creamed spinach, and roasted tomatoes.

The salad was in the refrigerator, the ingredients for the creamed spinach ready to be combined on the stove top, and the pheasant and tomatoes prepared and ready to slide into the oven as soon as Connor got back.

She looked at her watch. Six-thirty. Where was he? His meeting with out-of-town clients must be running late.

She wondered whether she had time to run out before he got back. Most of the groceries she needed could wait for tomorrow, but she'd discovered an hour ago that she was a few ingredients short for the pie she'd been planning to make for dessert.

She glanced at her watch again and bit her lip. She could dash out to the supermarket and be back in no time. Connor wouldn't even have to know.

Her mind made up, she grabbed a sheet of paper and scribbled a note just in case Connor got back before she did: "Out to the supermarket. Back soon." She used tape to attach the note to the mirror by the front door, then grabbed her purse.

As she'd thought, it took her no time at all to get to the supermarket and through the check-out line. The rain meant the store was more empty than usual.

When she got outside again, the rain had stopped,

but the overcast sky and fog made everything look dreary and dark.

She started across the parking lot to her car, juggling her two bags and purse.

Spotting her car, she noticed again that the new paint job—which had cost a mint—had fortunately covered up the graffiti that had been spray-painted several weeks ago.

Something looked strange however. Drawing closer, she realized the back of the car was tilting downward.

Darn. Had she gotten a flat?

Dropping her bags on the ground, she walked between her car and the one parked next to it and bent to inspect her back tire.

A clean slice through the rubber.

Her heart began to thud.

Someone had slashed her tire.

She heard a car coming toward her and automatically straightened up.

A gunshot sounded, followed quickly by another. She ducked just as the windshield of her car cracked and splintered.

Her mind raced frantically as she tried to figure a way out of the situation. Whoever had fired the bullets had sped past her, but that didn't mean he wouldn't be turning his car around for another pass.

She straightened up a little, risking a glance over her

car to try to get a look at the color and model of car that the gunman was driving, but didn't see anything.

"Help! Someone call the police!" she screamed even as she dug into her purse for her cell phone.

At the sound of feet pounding the pavement, she crouched down.

"Allison! For God's sake, stay down!"

It was Connor's voice shouting to her as he seemed to run past, even as she heard a car speed out of the parking lot with a shriek of tires.

"Dammit!" Connor said.

He cursed some more as Allison heard him coming back toward her.

She straightened, pushing her hair out of her face, and stepped from between the parked cars.

"I tried to get a shot at him, but he was too far away," Connor said, breathing heavily.

Her eyes shot downward and she gaped as she noticed the gun that Connor grasped in his hand. Where had *that* come from?

When her gaze moved upward again, she focused for the first time on the expression on Connor's face.

He looked mad as hell.

Seven

While they drove back to the townhouse, Connor kept a grip on his temper. But only because he had to.

They'd just finished talking to the police, who'd recovered a couple of unusual-looking bullets—or slugs, in police lingo—from the scene around the parking lot. With any luck, the police would have a theory soon on the caliber and model of gun that the perpetrator had probably used in the shooting.

Unfortunately, the parking lot—at least the part around Allison's car—had been empty of people at the time of the shooting, probably due in no small part to the bad weather. Of the two people whom the police had interviewed who had seen the perp's car speed away, one had sworn the car was gray while the other had called it blue.

In any case, Connor doubted that the gunman was stupid enough to use a vehicle with plates that could be easily traced back to him, though he'd make sure that the police and his own people nevertheless looked into it.

And that was the other thing: the profile of Allison's unknown harasser that he and Allison had constructed could be thrown out the window.

The assailant had now done more than merely threaten and vandalize property. He'd shown he was desperate enough to try a direct attack on Allison. Not only that, but, chillingly, he'd apparently slashed Allison's tire before the shooting in order to make it hard for her to flee by car.

Still, Connor wasn't convinced that the signs pointed to a member of Taylor's gang rather than a white-collar criminal such as Kendall. Allison's assailant had proved—fortunately—not to have very good aim. While it was possible that the incident in the parking lot had been intended as a gang-inspired drive-by shooting, the fact that the job had been so botched raised questions in Connor's mind.

The minute he'd gotten back to the townhouse and found the note Allison had left behind, he'd taken off after her, trying to reach her on her cell phone and not succeeding. When he'd gotten to the parking lot, he'd pulled up right at the curb in front of the supermarket. He'd been getting out of his car when he'd heard the first shot ring out. Icy fear had wrapped itself around his heart as he'd reached for his own gun.

He gave a quick glance at Allison sitting in the passenger seat next to him. She sat looking straight ahead, still appearing shaken by what had transpired in the last couple of hours.

Silence reigned between them until they got into the townhouse. At which point, Connor decided it was time to get some answers. "I have a distinct memory of telling you to stay put," he said tightly. "Correct me if I'm wrong, but running out to the supermarket does not count as staying put."

"You were delayed," she responded, irritation lacing her voice. "And, anyway, I refuse to be a prisoner in my own home."

"Right," he said harshly as he followed her into the living room. "It appears you'd rather be dead."

She stopped and whirled back to face him, temper flaring in her eyes. "That's blunt," she fired back. "Anyway, even if you'd been with me, I might still have gotten shot at."

"True, but it's all about the odds, princess, and it would have been less likely," he snarled back. "He, or whoever it was who took a shot at you, would have thought twice about it if you looked as if you had security."

"Since when do you carry a gun?" she demanded abruptly.

"What do you think being in the security business means, petunia?" he said, his tone scornful. "Of course I've got a gun."

He didn't add that he was considered an excellent shot, keeping his skills honed at a shooting range. His clients expected him to provide top-notch security and that included using a gun if necessary. Fortunately, it had never been necessary—until today—because he was adept at using other means to get results.

"And I can't believe you chased that nut," she continued. "You could have been killed!"

Worried about him, was she? Under different circumstances, he'd have been pleased, but right now he was still furious about the way she'd completely disregarded his instructions. "So why did you run out?" he asked. "What was so important you couldn't wait for me to get back? Or give me a call on my cell, for God's sake?"

She went still, looking away, then glancing back. She appeared embarrassed, though that didn't make sense. "What?"

"I was planning a romantic dinner," she said finally. "For two. I needed some ingredients."

Her admission floored him. That was it? That was the important errand she'd told the police she'd had to run? He'd have been happy munching on cardboard if it had kept her inside!

The only good thing that had come out of the shooting was that the police would now be stationed outside the townhouse whenever Allison was home. They were taking the threats against her even more seriously.

Still, Allison's admission brought home an unpleasant truth: they'd both gotten more focused on exploring the new-found physical chemistry between them than on keeping her safe.

Instead of thinking of him as a bodyguard whose orders should be followed to a T, Allison had been thinking of him as a lover who wouldn't necessarily get furious with her for disregarding what he'd said. She'd gone out and risked her life because she'd been planning to surprise him with a romantic dinner, for God's sake!

For his part, as much as he'd tried to convince himself otherwise, sleeping with her had changed everything. He wasn't the cool-headed expert he needed to be in dangerous situations. Instead, he was running on emotion because the thought of anything happening to her tied him up in knots.

Aloud, he said, "That's it? You ran out to the store so you could cook dinner?" He raked his fingers through his hair. "Where was your judgment?"

She folded her arms. "Obviously, in the wrong place," she said sarcastically, "if I was thinking of cooking dinner for you. Clearly I was wasting my time."

Anger battled with relief inside him. "You're still the rash, headstrong princess, aren't you? When are you going to learn to think before you act?"

"Well, I'm thinking now," she said coldly, dropping her arms. "And what I'm thinking is that taking our relationship to a new level was a mistake." She flashed him a look of disdain. "I should have known."

She should have known? Heck, *he* should have known. He should have known better than to get involved with her.

He and Allison came from different worlds and he was a fool to have forgotten that for even a minute. She was the sheltered daughter of a wealthy family and he'd always be the guy who climbed out of rough-and-tumble, blue-collar South Boston.

Even after Harvard, even after more than ten years building a multimillion-dollar business, he was still rough around the edges. His South Boston accent trickled in when he wasn't careful. And, frankly, he didn't blend with the country-club set and never would.

Still, the fact that she'd brought up their different backgrounds in an argument riled him. "You can try chalking me up as a mistake," he said silkily, "but we're dynamite in bed together."

"Go to—"

"I'm betting," he said, cutting her off, "that the pretty boys over at the country club haven't done nearly as good a job of satisfying you, have they, petunia? Otherwise you wouldn't still be looking for a roll in the sack with a guy who's seen the seedier side of life."

Her face had gone pale with anger. "That's right, Rafferty, and I'm glad you realized it, because that's all you were. A nice little frolic," she said, her voice haughty with disdain, "but certainly not someone I'd contemplate having a real relationship with."

He grabbed her arm as she stalked by him, whirling her to face him, but she shrugged off his hand.

"Give it up!" she said, her eyes flashing.

Ignoring her request, he followed her down the corridor toward the back of the house. They weren't done, not by a long shot. That she'd even try to dismiss him as nothing more than a quick fling had him seething.

Entering the kitchen, she went over to the sink.

"Dammit, we're not done."

"Oh, we're done all right," she said without turning around, starting to rinse a glass. "Done, over, finished."

He laughed derisively. "If you believe that, petunia, then leprechauns live at the end of the rainbow."

"What I believe, Rafferty," she said, turning around, "is that you need to cool off!"

A spray of cold water hit him square in the face before he could react. "What the—!" Raising his arms to shield his face, he stalked toward her.

They wrestled with the hose from the sink, water dousing them both, until he was able to yank the nozzle out of her hand.

He was about to let her know exactly what he thought but then his gaze dropped a notch, connecting with the front of her white shirt, which was plastered to her, her nipples clearly visible through the clingy fabric of her wet bra and shirt.

His blood heated.

She raised her arms to shield herself.

"Don't," he muttered.

She went still. "Damn you, Rafferty," she whispered. "I don't want this."

He raised his gaze, meeting her eyes. "Whether we want it or not seems almost beside the point," he said in a bemused voice. "It's there between us and always has been."

She tossed her head, wet strands of hair sending droplets onto them both. "I don't know what you mean."

"Liar," he chided softly, moving before her.

They were practically toe-to-toe now. He let his eyes drop down to her mouth, which parted on a soft breath.

"That's right, darling," he taunted. "Let me see how you feel."

Her eyes sparked fire. "Go to—"

His head swooped down then and he swallowed

the end of her sentence in a kiss that was searing and desperate—as searing and desperate and hot as his need for her.

He was still running on the remnants of the adrenaline that had started earlier in the parking lot, except that now the reality of their near brush with death, mixed with relief, was channeling that energy into a need for sexual release. Even understanding what was provoking him, however, was not enough for his intellect to overcome his baser instincts.

She moaned in his arms, meeting him kiss for desperate kiss, her hands tangling in his hair, anchoring him.

He lifted her up onto the kitchen counter, sandwiching himself between her legs as her skirt rode high on her thighs.

The need to affirm life, to stamp her as his, was overwhelming.

Hot mouth met hot mouth in desperate, soul-stirring kisses. He hungered to be inside her, to give vent to his frustration by seeking the release he knew awaited him there.

He lifted his head and yanked her shirt out of the waistband of her skirt, popping the buttons on the front of the garment in his haste to rid her of it.

When he'd peeled the shirt off of her, he bent his head to close his mouth over the peak of one breast through the fabric of her bra.

She made a sound that came out as half laugh, half gasp. "Connor!"

He shifted his mouth to her other breast, his hand at her back to urge her forward toward his mouth.

He felt her fingers threading through his hair, her breath coming rapidly. "Please," she gasped.

Her need inflamed him.

Raising his head, he let her tug him back to her as she pulled at the bottom of his shirt to loosen it from his jeans.

Their movements were jerky and desperate as they both attempted to rid him of his wet shirt.

As the shirt dropped to the floor, he realized they weren't going to be able to wait much longer. "Hang on," he said roughly, unsnapping his jeans and tugging the zipper downward.

"Yes," she said breathlessly.

He fumbled with a foil packet from his wallet. Then his fingers pushed aside her underwear. Testing and finding her warm and wet, he groaned.

"Connor," she said, her voice cloudy with passion.

He shifted, pulling her forward to the edge of the counter, and then over, sliding her down on him even as he pushed upward.

She gasped. "Please, yes."

He took up a rhythm then, abandoning himself to turbulent sensation and fiery passion as she clung to him, her legs wrapped around him, her head nestled in the curve of his shoulder and her breathing rapid.

His muscles strained, and his breathing grew more labored as the tension mounted. She moaned, and arched in his arms.

Their mutual release when it came was quick and powerful. He felt her tense, gasp, call his name, seconds before he lost himself in oblivion.

Tap, tap, tap. Realizing she'd again been lost in thought, Allison put down the pencil she'd been tapping against the desk that she sometimes called hers in the District Attorney's Office.

The events of Saturday night replayed themselves in her mind.

What had he called her? *A rash, headstrong princess.*

How dare he! He'd spoken and acted as if he thought she hadn't changed much, as if she were— still—a naive, wayward teenager. Even now, having a deeper appreciation for how his protective instincts had developed, she couldn't excuse how he'd dismissively labeld her

His words and actions rankled all the more because this time, instead of merely visiting a bar because she harbored a secret crush on him, she'd actually slept with him. She'd let him strip her bare both physically and emotionally. The betrayal this time was oh so much worse.

She'd begun to think they had a new understanding, one based on mutual respect. Instead, he'd apparently been thinking of her as nothing more than a spoiled little heiress, albeit one with whom he enjoyed amazing chemistry.

In fact, after the shooting, he'd acted just like her family with his overprotectiveness. He'd lit into her as if she were still an underage teenager lacking judgment.

Her lips tightened reflexively.

Their relationship—however short-lived—had been a mistake. Of that, she was now certain. There was no way they could have a real relationship—one based on mutual trust and respect—when he'd made it clear he saw her as nothing more than a sheltered and pampered princess.

She'd been insane to have been planning to welcome him home with a romantic dinner. Ironically, thanks to their argument, she now agreed with him about going out for ingredients for dessert.

She should have nuked some macaroni and cheese, slid a bowl at him, and told him that he was dining in style. Or, better yet, handed him a spoon and invited him to enjoy the stuff directly from a can.

Men were such animals.

Speaking of which…her face burned as she recalled the frenzied interlude on the kitchen counter that had followed their argument.

She should have kneed him and walked away. Instead, a combustible combination of relief at having escaped unharmed and anger at him had led to sizzling sex—as if Connor needed any further evidence that, if nothing else, they were great lovers.

She wondered at the reference he'd made to the attraction that had always been between them. Could he have known about her teenaged infatuation with him? Did he know she'd been in the bar that night in the hope of seeing him?

At least she hadn't admitted her teenaged infatuation to him. That would have made her humiliation complete.

Her phone rang, startling her out of her thoughts. Picking up the receiver, she said, "Hello?"

"Allison!"

"Hello, Quentin." She made her voice cool. Her brother was still on her less-than-wonderful persons list.

"Thank God you're okay!"

Someone had obviously spilled the beans to Quentin about Saturday's incident—the details of which had miraculously stayed out of the newspapers— and she had a good idea who that someone was. She sighed. "Yes, I'm fine. No need to worry."

"No need to worry?" Quentin said, sounding uncharacteristically agitated. "Are you crazy? You could have been killed and that's all you have to say?"

"Well, as you can tell, I wasn't. So, sorry to say, your younger sister is still here to torment you."

"Quit it with the glibness, Ally," her brother said impatiently. "You're just lucky Mom and Dad are in Europe on vacation at the moment and Noah and Matt are on business trips. Otherwise, they'd all be descending on you."

"Don't I know it," she muttered.

"What?"

"Nothing."

"Heck, I'd have been there myself if I didn't have some VIPs coming into the office this morning," Quentin said. "Anyway, Connor assured me that he has everything under control."

Her hand tightened on the receiver. "Oh, he did, did he?"

She heard Quentin sigh. "Allison, for the love of God, would you just try listening to Connor for a change? I know you two can barely stand each other—"

She wondered what Quentin's reaction would have been if he'd known she and Connor had recently found one area where they *could* deal with each other.

"—but he's there to protect you," Quentin continued, "and he's one of the best in the business. So would you quit trying to make the guy's job harder than it has to be?"

"And I still have a job to do, Quentin," she said, her tone clipped, "and that's putting the baddies behind bars. Unfortunately, that may involve some risks."

"Right and that's another thing." Quentin paused and cleared his throat, seeming to choose his words carefully. "Have you thought about what you're going to do after the DA's Office? You've been there, what? Four or five years?"

"Close to five. But who's counting when you're having fun?"

"I don't think the family can take much more of this, Allison. This latest episode with your getting shot at may be the nail in the coffin for Mom and Dad."

She closed her eyes. "You've told them?"

"Not yet, but *someone* has to because the papers may link your name to the shooting sooner or later," he said significantly.

She opened her eyes again. "Fine, I know." She could already picture the newspaper headlines. Years of hard work trying to stake an identity for herself apart from her well-known family would evaporate before her eyes.

"All I'm saying is you may want to start thinking about when this stint at the DA's Office is going to end. It's just too dangerous. Connor said the usual stint is three years or so."

Connor had said that, had he? She'd be interested in knowing what else Connor had said. "Maybe it isn't just a stint. Have you thought about that? Maybe I want to climb the ladder at the DA's Office."

Quentin didn't say anything but a distinct sigh came over the line.

"Besides," she persisted, "I'm not the only one taking risks, Quentin. Everyone in the office has a tough job. If it weren't me, it'd be someone else."

"All right, that's all praiseworthy and good, but the fact of the matter is that it *is* you," Quentin argued. "*You've* been the one getting threats. *You've* been the one getting shot at. And, you can't tell me that your name and your family's wealth and high profile don't put you at special risk."

She thought about the phone threat she'd gotten: kidnapped and held "for a pretty penny." Quentin had inadvertently hit the mark. Aloud, she said, "I'm not going to be boxed in by a whole set of rules just because of my last name."

Quentin started to interrupt, but she went on, "And you can tell your friend Connor not to worry. I won't be trying to cook dinner for him again anytime soon."

If it were possible, she was even more annoyed with Connor by the time she got off the phone.

Ratted her out to her family again, had he? He

hadn't even waited for her to tell them in her own way. Instead, he'd lost no time in spilling the entire story to Quentin as if she were still a recalcitrant teen whose family he had to enlist to keep her in line.

Had he also had the gall to suggest to Quentin that she should be looking to move on from the DA's Office because the prosecutor's job had become too dangerous for her? Is that how the thought had occurred to Quentin?

She wouldn't put it past Connor.

She narrowed her eyes. If Connor thought things were icy between them now, she fumed, he'd better get ready for a deep freeze.

Eight

Connor faced the mirror and attempted once again to work his tuxedo tie into a knot.

For the past week, he and Allison had avoided each other as much as it was possible to while still living under the same roof. That had not been as hard to accomplish as it might otherwise have been, since she'd been working late all week. As a result, he'd been able to catch up on things at the office and schedule some evening meetings.

Yet, the tension between them continued to mount, despite—or maybe because of—the fact he was back to sleeping in the bedroom down the hall from hers. He was still furious with her, but he was also suffering from a serious bout of sexual frustration.

They were like two tigers circling each other in the cage. And, unfortunately, their days of circling were about to come to an end.

Tonight was the Cortland Ball, and even he knew it was the biggest and oldest charity ball of the Boston social season.

Usually he avoided such events like the plague. His company was well-known enough that he didn't have to hobnob with the rich and snooty. Business came to him.

But the Whittaker Foundation was one of the major sponsors of the Cortland Ball this year, so Allison had to attend. And if Allison had to attend, *he* had to attend.

Even if they were barely on speaking terms. Even if his damned bow tie was choking him, he thought irritably, running his finger around inside the collar of his shirt now that he had worked his tie into a perfect if slightly too-tight knot. He left his bedroom and headed downstairs.

The one perk to attending this shindig was that Hugh Kendall, the indicted business executive Allison was prosecuting, would be there. It would be a first-class opportunity to study one of the prime suspects in the threats against Allison.

When Connor got downstairs to the front hall, he

checked his cell-phone messages again and resigned himself to waiting for Allison to come down the stairs.

Ten minutes later, a small sound alerted him to her presence moments before he glanced up. When he did, the sight of her stole his breath away.

She was wrapped in a strapless, sky-blue sheath that hugged all the right curves. The style of her hair, piled high on her head—thanks to the work of the stylist who had come to the door earlier—further accentuated her elegant décolletage.

As she came down the stairs, the deep slit in her gown parted like a curtain to reveal shapely legs and feet shod in silver, high-heeled pumps. She clutched a small silver purse in one hand and jewels glittered at her ears and wrist.

Diamonds, he noted with the modicum of his brain not given over to carnal lust. Yet her neck was bare.

If they'd been married, he thought, and preparing for tonight, he'd have given her diamonds to adorn her neck, too. He'd have trailed kisses along her neck, across her collarbone, and down to the cleavage revealed by the heart-shaped neckline of her gown. Eexactly, he realized, as her ensemble was designed to encourage him—or more precisely, any red-blooded male—to do.

She looked every inch the princess that he often taunted her as being. Except, instead of conjuring the mockery he often made a pretense of exhibiting, he felt every fiber within him tense with elemental attraction.

As she neared the last step, he mentally shook himself and held out his hand to her.

Her eyes flashed fire, but she let him assist her the rest of the way. And while the expression on her face said she was still displeased with him, her heightened color also said she was not immune to the physical attraction between them either.

He'd been pleased when she'd told him that she didn't have an escort for tonight. If she'd had one, he had a hunch he'd have wanted to rip the guy apart.

She arched a brow. "Looked your fill?" she asked tartly, her chin coming up.

"For that I'd have to peel you out of that gown," he parried, knowing his words would rile her.

"Then you'll be looking for a very long time," she said frostily, opening the door to the hall closet and retrieving a wrap. "And if your eyelids are liable to be glued open all night, I hope you're bringing along some eye drops."

"Why don't you carry a bottle of the stuff for me?" he asked lazily. "Then when I'm afflicted—as I inevitably will be because I *intend* to watch you all evening, princess—you can come minister to me."

She closed the closet door with a thud, wrap in hand. "The only way I'll be ministering to you is with a swift kick in the—"

"Tut-tut," he interrupted, now thoroughly enjoying himself. "This is a charity ball, remember? And isn't charity supposed to begin at home?"

"Here's a news flash for you, Rafferty, in case the message hasn't gotten through to that iron-plated ego of yours," she said, yanking open the front door and then stopping abruptly without going out. "I haven't exactly been feeling charitable toward you lately."

When they arrived at the Riverton Ballroom, where the gala was being held, Connor noted Allison lost no time in breaking away from him in order to mingle with the other guests during the predinner cocktail hour. She seemed to know most of the people there and socialized easily.

And why not? he thought. She'd grown up in this world.

Seeing her in her natural milieu underscored the differences in their backgrounds. He'd been furious when she'd thrown those differences back at him in the heat of their argument, but, if ever he was tempted to agree with her that those differences doomed a relationship between them, now would be the time.

He sipped from his wineglass and watched as Allison smiled and nodded at one of the male guests. The bland-as-a-vanilla-wafer jerk was looking at her as if she were an ornament he was planning to hang on his illustrious family tree.

Sloan, his name was, if Connor remembered the face correctly. A member of the Makepeace family, listed in the Social Register and tracing its lineage back to the *Mayflower*—as any good Boston Brahmin family would.

Connor's lips twisted as he watched Sloan Makepeace lean toward Allison.

Then he caught himself. He had a job tonight and it wasn't ogling Allison. Oh, he intended to keep his eyes on her, all right, just as he'd said, but that was only to make sure she stayed safe and stayed *put*.

Connor took another sip of his wine and scanned the room—just in time to catch sight of Hugh Kendall making an appearance at one of the doorways to the ballroom.

The businessman looked shorter and stockier than he had in the pictures Connor had seen of him in the papers. He was definitely balding, though, around fifty, and no more than medium height.

Connor watched as Kendall and his date—a grand dame of the Boston social scene—moved among the guests. If the news reports were right, Kendall's decade-long marriage had ended several years ago and he had since become a popular man-about-town, squiring socialites to high-profile events.

A sycophantic prig, he thought. Allison was right. Kendall's social standing was clearly essential to him. If the allegations of embezzlement stuck, he would be ruined. Not only would he be heading to prison, but he'd be an outcast from the upper crust.

For all his posturing, Kendall had little more than his money to gain him entry to events such as the Cortland Ball.

Connor had done some digging and he knew Kendall neither came from an old-line family nor shared old prep-school ties with the people here tonight.

According to his investigation, Kendall had grown up in an upper-middle-class family in New Hampshire and had attended public schools before graduating from college with a business degree and moving to Boston to start his ascent in the business world.

Connor glanced over at Allison and noted she'd also marked Kendall's arrival. He knew without asking, however, that she would avoid Kendall. It would be improper for a prosecutor to be talking to a defendant in one of her cases.

On the other hand, Connor reflected, Kendall looked at ease despite the fact that nearly everyone there tonight must know he'd had the audacity to show up even though Allison, who was prosecuting his case, would be present.

Connor narrowed his eyes. If Kendall was their man, then Allison's harasser was a cool cucumber. Exactly the type who would be hard to catch. And exactly the type he intended to watch like a hawk.

* * *

Allison glanced around the ballroom. She'd managed to shake Connor for the time being. Unfortunately, though, her parents were bearing down on her. She braced herself as they approached. "Hello, Mom."

"Ally." Her mother leaned in for a kiss before drawing back and looking searchingly at her face, concern etched on hers. "How are you feeling? Are you having any trouble sleeping? Because if you are—"

"Mom, I'm fine." She'd spoken with her parents earlier in the week about the shooting incident, but she'd spared them the details, which would just have worried them needlessly.

Her parents exchanged looks. Her father was an older version of Quentin, but his dark hair was peppered with gray, giving him a distinguished look.

"You should have told us you'd received another death threat in the mail just days before the shooting," her father said gravely.

Allison suppressed her irritation. Connor, it seemed, had been talking again. "I didn't want to worry you and Mom unnecessarily," she said, hoping the explanation was one they'd be satisfied with. "You were on a business trip hundreds of miles away last week. There was nothing you could do except worry even more than you'd already been doing."

"Of course we would have worried!" her mother exclaimed.

Allison took a deep breath. "Thanks to Quentin, I have a bodyguard, remember? I'm taking precautions."

"Connor said that you'd gone out without him when you were attacked," her father countered.

Snitch. What else had he told her parents? All she needed in order to make her humiliation complete was for Connor to have divulged the reason she'd left the house. Aloud, she said, "Connor has been saying a lot these days." She turned as Quentin parted from Liz, who was speaking to another woman, and strolled up to join them. "What else has Connor been saying, Quent?"

Quentin held up his hands. "Hey, he's only trying to help."

"I thought I was just getting a bodyguard," she said indignantly, "but, apparently, Connor is doing double duty as a spy."

"Now, Allison—"

"You should have warned me, Quent. If I'd known Connor was reporting everything to you and the rest of the family, I'd at least have given him something interesting to relay. You know, wild parties, dancing on tables, men swinging from the chandelier…male strippers…"

"Actually," Quentin said dryly, "getting information out of Connor is like prying open a clam with your bare hands."

"Oh, come on." She cocked her head. "Are you

going to deny he lost no time telling you about the shooting incident last week? Even before I had the chance to pick up the phone?"

Quentin frowned. "Only because I phoned him and demanded to know what the heck had happened the night before. I had gotten a call from the police to let me know that they were going to do everything possible to try to keep the tabloid journalists at bay about the shooting. One of the nice things about being a major donor to police charities is that the police brass remembers you when, say, your sister is involved in a shooting." Quentin paused and gave her a meaningful look. "Naturally, I had to ask *what* shooting."

"I was going to call you," she said, knowing she sounded a bit defensive. The truth was she hadn't been relishing that conversation with her brother— or any other member of her family for that matter. She knew her family well enough to know their reactions would have fallen somewhere between alarm and panic, and she hadn't been wrong.

"After I got a call from the police," Quentin added, "I phoned Connor."

"Don't you mean interrogated?" she asked, her annoyance coming through in her tone. "And why didn't you bother to call me first?"

"Because," Quentin said patiently, "given a choice between the two of you, I knew I'd have a better shot with hin at getting the straight story."

She crossed her arms. "Are you saying I would have lied?"

Her brother gave her a knowing look. "Artful omission is more like it."

Allison dropped her arms in exasperation. "Whatever."

"And, yes, believe it or not, I did have to threaten and cajole Connor," Quentin went on. "He initially told me to call *you*. I think the only reason he eventually said anything at all was that I'd already found out more or less what happened from the police."

So maybe Connor hadn't gone racing to her brother with the news.

"I must say, I agree with Quentin," her mother put in. "Connor seemed very reluctant to go into much detail about the shooting when your father and I asked him about it. Frankly, I think he wanted to spare us unnecessary worry."

"And, by the way," her father added, "Connor is not the one who told us about the threat you'd received in the mail. That was something that the police mentioned to Quentin when they called him."

She looked across the ballroom and her eyes met Connor's. The look on his face said he was debating whether to walk over. She shook her head almost imperceptibly. She didn't need his help handling her family.

She did owe him an apology though—at least for

jumping to the conclusion that he'd raced to her family to blab about the shooting.

Sitting next to Connor at dinner was torture, Allison thought. Her family, fortunately, was sitting among guests at other tables. Otherwise, it would have been much harder to pretend interest in the mundane chitchat being carried on at her table.

She took another bite of her dessert. Mercifully, the guest on her left had just excused himself to say hello to people he knew at another table.

She itched to hash things out with Connor. She wanted to apologize, yes. At the same time, though, she was still piqued about the high-handed way he'd acted after the attack in the parking lot. Surely he owed her an apology as well?

She stole a look at him. He was chatting with the guest on his right, the wife of a Congressman. Connor's slightly rough-around-the-edges quality was set off tonight by his tuxedo. The juxtaposition was incredibly sexy and, she noted sourly, apparently appreciated by the Congressman's wife as well.

The stab of jealousy brought her up short. She was spared having to analyze the emotion, however, because Connor took that moment to turn to her.

"Dance with me?" he asked. His lips were curved upward but his tone was mocking. "I think we can survive it, don't you?" He nodded around their table at the empty seats and the couple getting up at the other end. "Besides, it will look odd if we didn't take at least one turn around the room."

She nodded and let him help her rise from her seat. The dance floor might finally afford her the opportunity and privacy to get her apology over with.

When they were out on the dance floor, he drew her to him for the start of a slow song. If she'd been dispassionate, she would have said his touch felt light but firm. But, since she was far from feeling detached, his touch—from their bodies brushing to his hand at her back guiding her—was causing waves of pulsating sensation to radiate outward from the points of contact.

For a while, they danced without speaking, gliding across the dance floor to a slow and sweet song until the temptation to rest her head on his shoulder became palpable.

She gave herself a mental shake. She had things to say to him and she'd better get on with it.

Before she could say anything, however, he stirred the hair at her temple with his breath and murmured, "Silence becomes you."

She looked up with a start and saw the mocking laughter in his eyes. She'd been practically swooning in his arms—while thinking that she had to apologize to him—and he was mocking her! She decided the apology she owed him could wait a little longer.

"Humility would become you but I don't see you exhibiting any."

"That's my girl." He had the nerve to laugh outright. "I was wondering where that temper of yours had gone. You seemed as deflated as a dead balloon during dinner."

Well, Allison thought, so much for her attempt at seeming at ease during dinner. "Quite the one for compliments tonight, aren't you?"

"Is that what you want? Compliments?" he asked. Though his tone was still mocking, it contained a hint of seriousness.

"Don't be ridiculous."

He cocked his head, pretending to think, before clearing his throat and looking down at her. "Your eyes have the color and sparkle of aquamarines, your hair the darkness and luster of a night sky—"

"Stop." Even knowing he was teasing, his words sent a ripple of liquid pleasure through her.

"Why?"

"Because we're in a room full of people." And she couldn't take anymore.

"Ah." His eyes gleamed. "Haven't you ever heard that dancing is the vertical expression of a horizontal desire?"

He was telling her? She was practically going up in flames, incensed yet aroused by their banter.

"So how am I doing? Am I as good as Slade?"

"Who?"

"Preppy boy."

She must have continued to wear a blank look, because he added impatiently, "Mr. Make-Love-Not-War."

"That's Makepeace," she said, correcting him.

"Same thing."

"And his name is Sloan, not Slade."

"Yeah, whatever. Were Makepeace's compliments as good?" He leaned closer to whisper in her ear. "I bet he didn't turn you on, petunia."

He was impossible. Forget the apology. She figured he owed *her* one by this point, but she was willing to consider the two of them even if it meant she could get rid of him *now*.

His lips turned up a notch. "The look on your face is saying you want to kick me in the shins."

"And some other places."

"You're too fiery for a milksop like Makepeace."

The song they were dancing to faded into another slow tune. "I'll be the judge of that."

Connor cast her a disbelieving look. "Seems to me you've already made up your mind. Otherwise, you wouldn't still have a thing for guys from the wrong side of the tracks."

One guy in particular, but she wasn't going to give him the satisfaction of knowing that. Especially since he seemed to be taking pleasure in baiting her.

"You know," she said, her voice dripping disdain, "I must have been crazy even to have thought I owed you an apology."

She had the satisfaction of seeing him look taken aback for an instant. That expression was quickly replaced by one of sardonic amusement however. "I can think of many reasons why you'd owe me an apology, petunia. So why don't you narrow it down for me and tell me what in particular spurred this fit of remorse?"

She gritted her teeth. The only remorse she was feeling at the moment was at not having clobbered him. But, instead, she said, "I got a call from Quentin on the morning after the incident in the parking lot. He seemed to know all about what had happened without my telling him."

"So naturally you thought I was the one who called to fill him in," he supplied.

"It was a logical assumption to have jumped to under the circumstances," she said defensively.

He arched a brow. "Logical because I'm an untrustworthy snitch where you're concerned, is that it?" His lips tightened. "Ever since I lied to you and went to your folks with the story of you at the biker bar when you were seventeen. It goes as far back as that, doesn't it?"

"It wasn't a far-fetched conclusion to jump to," she asserted again. "Anyway, are you also going to deny suggesting to Quentin that I quit the DA's Office because the job may have become too dangerous for me?"

"I didn't suggest it to him. He brought it up." He gave her a considering look, then added, "But I won't say I disagree."

Her temper flared. Fortunately, the song they were dancing to faded away and the band decided to take a break.

She pulled out of Connor's hold. "Great, then the sooner we find out who's been making the threats, the sooner my job will stop being so dangerous and the sooner *you* can get the heck out of my house. Frankly, it won't be a moment too soon for my taste. On either count."

She turned on her heel, not giving him a chance to respond, though she noted that his face had tightened with anger.

Of all the nerve. She'd been a lovesick fool to think something unique and lasting had been developing between them. Instead of giving her his respect, it was clear that to him, she'd always be a spoiled little rich girl who needed protection. *His* protection.

Nine

It was Saturday, the day of the annual Memorial Day Weekend barbecue at Allison's parents' house.

Usually Connor looked forward to this Whittaker family tradition. Usually, but not this year.

Last year, according to what had since become Whittaker family lore, the barbecue had marked the kickoff of Quentin and Elizabeth's whirlwind relationship. Allison had made her famous suggestion that her brother act as her best friend's sperm donor. Now, one year later, Connor's old college buddy was happily married to Liz and the father of newborn Nicholas.

Connor took a swig of his beer and chanced a

glance across the lawn at the cause of his dour mood. Allison was cuddling baby Nicholas in her arms, making cooing noises. The baby must have done something unexpectedly funny because she looked up, laughing, and their eyes met.

She looked away quickly, but not before a yearning so strong it hurt slammed into him. It wasn't a pure physical need for her, he realized. It was deeper, more powerful. A vision of her cradling their own baby flashed across his mind.

Then he pulled himself up short. She was tying him up in knots and it had to stop. Until they found out who was threatening her, he reminded himself, sorting out his relationship with Allison was on hold.

With any luck, though, the holding pattern wouldn't have to continue much longer. He felt for his cell phone again. No call yet, but there was time. Guests were still arriving at the Whittaker's house.

In the meantime, he thought self-deprecatingly, he could brood at leisure. The Cortland Ball had brought home for him that he and Allison were from different worlds. And, as furious as he still was about her tossing that in his face in the middle of an argument, he'd since acknowledged to himself that there was some validity to her point.

"Hey, Rafferty."

He turned and caught a volleyball just before it hit him in the stomach.

Noah Whittaker sauntered up, a grin on his face.

"Still greeting your guests with a sucker punch to the stomach?" Connor asked dryly.

"No, just you," Noah replied, then gave him another easy grin. "It's one of the rituals reserved for brothers, honorary or otherwise."

Since his college days, Connor acknowledged, he'd had an easy camaraderie with Noah, who had the reputation of being the most fun-loving of the Whittaker brothers.

"Stop doing your brooding James Dean impersonation and get your rear end moving," Noah continued. "There's a volleyball game starting up and we're beating Quentin and Matt's team again this year so I can claim bragging rights to a winning streak."

Connor tossed the volleyball back at him and asked wryly, "You mean so you can make it two years in a row?"

"Hey, you gotta start somewhere."

"Fine, I'm game." As he and Noah made their way to the back of the house, he figured volleyball was preferable to standing around ruminating over Allison.

Noah slanted him a look. "Allison's on our team. Is that cool with you?"

"Why wouldn't it be?" Just because he alternated between wanting to shake some sense into her and a desperate need to make passionate love to her didn't mean he couldn't play nice if the situation called for it.

"Don't know." Noah shrugged. "Maybe because you two singe everyone around you with the sparks you throw off when you're near each other. Heck, someone who didn't know you might think you two were crazy about each other."

Connor almost stopped in his tracks.

Noah's comment was startling, Connor realized, because it was true. He *was* crazy about Allison. Crazy in love with her. Not just want, not just desire. Love.

It was the right name for what he'd been feeling all along, he finally realized. And, if it was the last thing he did, he'd get her to admit she felt the same way about him. Then they could talk about their differences.

He couldn't change who he was and where he'd come from, but he loved her deeply and irrevocably. And if that still wasn't enough for her, well—his heart clenched—she could just try to find a guy who'd care for her more than he did.

Noah waved a hand in front of his eyes. "Hey, Rafferty, you still on Earth with the rest of us mortals?"

Connor knew Noah was expecting a flip response, so he said, "If it hasn't been apparent, your sister has been barely acknowledging my existence lately."

"You do know how to push her buttons, I'll give you that."

"Likewise, she's not so bad at pushing buttons herself."

Noah threw him an amused look. "Why don't you help take her off our hands?" he joked. "You know my parents think you're great. And, you'd be doing us a favor if you two got hitched."

Connor looked at Noah quizzically. He could swear there was a note of underlying seriousness to Noah's kidding but Noah's face revealed nothing other than his typical expression of amusement at the world. "If you value your health, you won't let Allison hear about that scheme."

As much as the Whittakers thought of him as family, Connor doubted any of them really regarded him as an ideal mate for the family's precious darling. No amount of polish would ever get rid of some of his rough edges.

Noah cast him a look of mock offense. "Me? Plotting to marry off Allison?"

Connor tossed him a skeptical look as they reached the volleyball net set up on a corner of the lawn in the Whittaker's backyard.

Noah sighed heavily as if being forced to confess. "Okay, yeah. Guilty." He shrugged, looking far from repentant. "Ever since Allison got ol' Quent hitched to Liz last year, I've suspected that she's set her sights on me and Matt. And, you know what they say, the best defense is a good offense."

"In other words," Connor supplied, playing along, "get her hitched to me before she gets you hitched?"

"Exactly." Noah added with a pretense of ruefulness, "Can't blame a guy for trying."

Connor looked over to see Allison joining the crowd near the net. "Yeah," he agreed, "but I'm not sure I'm good enough for our little princess."

Noah scoffed, dropping his teasing demeanor. "You're kidding, right? The folks adore you. They've never said it, but I think they'd be pleased if you and Allison ever wound up together. And, I've got to tell you, it would be a relief for me, Matt and Quentin." He gave a mock shudder. "Have you seen some of the guys Allison has brought home?"

Unfortunately, he had…and he agreed with Noah. He nodded over at Allison and said, "The princess might have some objections though."

Noah followed his gaze. "Yeah, I know Allison can get into her nose-in-the-air routine with you. But, I always thought that was just a defensive mechanism. You know, a way to show you that you don't get to her when you obviously do."

She showed him all right. Every opportunity she got. Aloud, he said, testing, "Just supposing I was willing to help you implement this little plot of yours—purely in the interest of helping you escape a possible marriage trap, of course—"

"Of course," Noah agreed readily.

"What's to say that you, Matt, and Quent don't beat me to a pulp for unintentionally breaking the princess's heart."

Noah cocked his head, pretending to consider that for a moment. "Okay, yeah, I grant you that's a risk. Under the circumstances, though," he said, his tone nonchalant, "I'd say it's more likely that the danger would be that the princess would break your heart."

Connor tossed him a quizzical look, but Noah's face revealed nothing. The youngest Whittaker brother, Connor thought, was way more depth than the fun-loving playboy the gossip columns portrayed him as.

Noah slapped him on the back. "Come on. We've got a game to play," he said, walking with him toward where the other players were standing, "and I can't wait to cream these guys."

As it turned out, their team eked out a victory for the second year in a row. Afterward, Connor sat down with a cold beer and some hot dogs. It was dusk and the party was starting to wind down.

He was just finishing his second hot dog when his cell phone rang. Sliding the phone out of his pocket, he noted that the name on the display was that of one of his top deputies.

He quickly excused himself and walked toward a nearby tree. No use getting the Whittakers' expectations up if the news wasn't what he hoped. He'd had a hunch, though, and had followed through on it.

The call was brief but nevertheless had him wanting to punch the air with satisfaction.

When he got back to the picnic table, he sat down next to Allison and, keeping his tone as mild as possible because he knew his words alone would be shocking enough, murmured, "They've caught Kendall."

She stopped in midmotion while reaching for a can of soda and swung to face him. "He's been arrested?"

He nodded. "And my guess is he'll be held without bail under the circumstances."

He watched as a variety of emotions flitted across her face. "Why?" she asked finally, seeming to settle on that one word as vague enough to encompass anything he might tell her.

Matt Whittaker glanced over at them from the other side of the table. "What's wrong?"

"Yeah," Noah chimed in, "you look pale, sis."

Connor looked down the table and noticed that they'd gotten Allison's parents' and Quent and Liz's attention, too.

It was just as well. He could get the story over with in one telling. "Hugh Kendall has been arrested in connection with the threats against Allison."

Liz gasped while Noah uttered an expletive that Connor privately agreed with. Then everybody tried to talk at once.

"How did the police catch him?" Allison's father

asked finally, making himself heard after the initial tumult had died down.

"The police executed a warrant and searched Kendall's house and car," Connor said. "They found a gun there that matches the type of .32-caliber weapon they think was used in the parking-lot shooting, based on the type of slugs they recovered that night."

"They executed a warrant? Based on what evidence?" Allison asked. She had been looking relieved since he'd told her the news, but now her tone was tinged with suspicion. "Were they able to trace the color of the car that the gunman used back to Kendall?"

"Does Kendall even have a state gun license?" Noah added.

Connor shook his head. "The answers to your questions are no and no. But, the police concluded that the slugs had probably come from a make of gun that hadn't been manufactured in a long time, so I decided to have my people do some more digging."

"Good going," Matt said, nodding approvingly.

"I had a couple of my investigators visit gun shops around Boston," Connor explained. "One shop owner recalled someone fitting Kendall's description asking about possibly *selling* some guns a while back. They were practically collector's items, and the guy who came in wanted to know how much they'd be worth."

Connor looked around the room. He had everyone's undivided attention, it seemed.

"None of the stuff I'd dug up on Kendall revealed that he was a gun enthusiast or even into hunting," he went on. "So, I figured, if Kendall did own some unlicensed guns and he was in fact the guy who had gone into the gun shop trying to sell some classic firearms, then he'd probably inherited some handguns. Once I had one of my investigators look into probate court records in New Hampshire, I knew we definitely had our man."

"How so?" asked Liz.

"Kendall's father's will is on file," he responded. "It reveals that he gave his gun collection to his son and that collection included the type of .32-caliber the police think was used in the shooting."

Connor looked at Allison and didn't add the fact that, since Kendall had kept the gun after the shooting, instead of disposing of the incriminating weapon, there was a good chance he was thinking of using it again, and to fatal effect.

The thought again sent chills down Connor's spine. As soon as all the clues had been gathered, he'd turned over his evidence to the police so a warrant could be executed. The urge first to beat the crap out of Kendall himself had been hard to resist however.

"What about the guy you saw lurking outside the townhouse that first night?" Allison asked. "Do you think it was Kendall who sped away that time?"

Connor nodded. "Probably. And, as we suspected,

Kendall was throwing us off the scent by making it seem as if the threats were coming from a run-of-the-mill hood."

"The note in the mail with the bad English you mean?" Allison asked.

Connor nodded. "Among other things."

"We all owe you a debt of gratitude, Connor," Allison's father said. "You know you're like family to us, but let us know if there's ever a way we can repay you."

Connor noted that, next to him, Allison stiffened slightly. "You mean on top of his hefty fees?" she asked.

Quentin shook his head. "Actually, I offered to pay him—" Quentin either ignored or didn't see the quelling look that Connor shot him "—but he refused. He insisted on volunteering his services."

Allison swiveled toward him and Connor met her look head-on. He could see what she was thinking. He'd purposely misled her. And this time he had no excuse.

"I'm relieved this episode is over," Ava Whittaker said. "It's been a painful and trying period for all of us."

"True, but if Ally continues to work at the DA's Office," Matt put in, "I guess we should all be prepared if she runs into another nut willing to take matters into his own hands."

"Speaking of which, how long *do* you intend to keep going at the DA's Office, Ally?" Noah asked.

Connor felt Allison tense next to him and saw Quent and Allison's parents exchange looks.

"You know, Allison," Ava said gently, as if knowing this was a sensitive subject, "you are at the point in your career when a lot of the Assistant DAs would be starting to think about their next job."

James Whittaker cast his daughter a sober look. "And, under the circumstances, you might want to think carefully about that."

"What circumstances, Dad?" Allison asked. "This was an isolated case of one disturbed individual attempting to intimidate and harass me." She shrugged. "It's not as if it hasn't happened to other prosecutors."

Quentin cleared his throat and spoke up. "We were all worried sick about you."

"Anyway, it's not as if the Assistant DA's job is the only potentially dangerous one in the world," Allison went on. "Mom is a family judge, but I don't see anyone here worried about one of the parties in her cases coming after her."

"That's because it hasn't happened," Quentin replied. "Whereas someone was firing bullets at you just a couple of weeks ago if you'll recall."

Connor sensed that Allison was reining in her temper with difficulty. "Maybe I want to rise through the ranks at the DA's Office, has anyone thought about that?" she demanded.

He wasn't known for his diplomacy, but Connor

nevertheless decided it was probably time that he stepped in. "Maybe we're not giving Allison the credit she's due."

Allison turned to look at him, the expression on her face saying she was wondering whether she'd heard him correctly.

Not glancing at her, he added, "I know I haven't."

"Thanks," Allison said from beside him, her tone tinged with surprise.

He addressed himself to all the Whittakers, who were exhibiting a range of emotions from quiet amusement to unmasked interest. "I've been with Allison night and day for the past several weeks," he said, hoping the Whittakers didn't take the "night and day" part too literally. "I've seen how tough she can be when the circumstances call for it."

Noah guffawed. "I'll say. And not just when the circumstances call for it, either."

From the corner of his eye, Connor saw Allison purse her lips.

Noah gave a mock shiver. "I rest my case."

"The truth is," Connor continued, "she refused to be cowed by the threats and she's certainly got the guts to be a prosecutor."

He looked at Allison, who was regarding him with questions in her eyes. He took a deep breath. "So, if Allison has set her sights on rising through the ranks at the DA's Office, I say more power to her."

Maybe it was because he'd finally acknowledged to himself that he loved her, but suddenly he was seeing the Whittakers through Allison's eyes. Her family knew she'd been performing a tough job well at the DA's Office, but none of them, it seemed, could get past some protective instincts where she was concerned.

And he'd been the most guilty of all. He'd unfairly been lumping her together with all the spoiled little rich girls he'd come to know, both through his security business and as an eligible and wealthy bachelor. It had been, he acknowledged, an easy way to keep her at an emotional distance and fight his perverse attraction to her.

Allison's brothers and sister-in-law looked thoughtful, while Allison's parents appeared similarly reflective.

Matt was the first to speak. "Connor has a point. We've all been thinking of Ally as someone we love and want to protect. Maybe that's blinded us to how tough and resilient she really is."

"We just wanted to make sure you didn't get hurt, sweetheart," Allison's father said. "Our intention wasn't to stifle you, but things may have gotten a little confused along the way."

"Yes," Ava agreed. "I'm sorry if we've come across as a bit heavy-handed sometimes, Ally. It's only because we love you."

"I guess if we're handing out apologies," Quentin added, "I should say ditto for me."

"If continuing to be a prosecutor is really what you want to do, we'll support you, of course," Ava said, looking at her husband for his concurring nod. "Naturally, the decision is yours. All we wanted was to make sure it was a well thought out decision."

Allison smiled at her mother. "Thanks, Mom."

Connor caught the quick look she sent his way before she added, "And try not to worry too much. Thanks to Connor, I've learned that maybe I should have been paying more attention to my personal safety."

She'd learned that, had she? Connor took some satisfaction in that. It would help when he was out of her house—and out of her life—again.

As the last of the guests were leaving, Allison was in the kitchen of her parents' house, packing up some food that the caterers had left behind. She looked up as her sister-in-law Liz approached.

"Hi," Liz said, picking up her purse and diaper bag from the kitchen counter. "Quentin and I were just about to depart." She stopped, giving Allison a searching look. "You look miserable."

"Thanks," she said wryly. She opened the refrigerator door and put some plastic containers inside.

Liz cocked her head as if contemplating something.

"Which is surprising when you think about it. I mean, Kendall has been caught. You should be ecstatic."

She should be, but she wasn't. She almost felt sorry for Kendall. She supposed the embezzlement allowed him to maintain a high-flying lifestyle. Having been born into a wealthy and connected family, however, she could have told him that wealth and fame could sometimes be a gilded cage.

But what was really bothering her was Connor. He'd helped catch Kendall. He'd defended her to her family. And now he was getting out of her life.

She should have been thrilled. Wasn't that what she'd told him she wanted?

Yet, Liz was right. She was miserable.

"And, because you look miserable, let me return a favor," Liz continued.

"What?"

"Last year you helped me realize that I shouldn't give up on Quentin, that Quentin loved me and all I needed to do was push a little more." She smiled. "So, I'm trying to return the favor."

Allison shrugged. "Thank you for making the effort, but, much as I hate to tell you, this is a whole different kettle of fish."

Liz laughed. "No, it's not. You just think it is because you're too deeply involved in it. You're exactly where I was last year."

Allison stared at her friend for a second. Last year,

after some prodding, Liz had admitted that she was in love with Quentin.

Liz was right. She herself wasn't just in danger of falling in love with Connor. She was head-over-heels, irrevocably, no-holds-barred in love.

Yet, Connor had announced that he'd be moving out of the townhouse this weekend and she'd just nodded mutely. If he loved her, would he be leaving?

She'd discovered that he'd insisted on not being paid for his security services. And he'd stayed by her side despite her attempts to get rid of him and despite the fact that he had no obligation to do so. She wanted to believe that meant something…but was she reading too much into it?

Quentin walked into the kitchen. "There you are," he said, giving his wife a gentle peck on the lips. "I've been looking for you. Are you ready to go?"

Liz smiled. "Yes, sorry to keep you waiting. Allison and I were just having a heart-to-heart."

"Oh, yeah?" Quentin asked. "What about?"

"Connor," Liz said simply.

"Ah."

"What do you mean 'ah'?" Allison asked. "And why did Connor insist on volunteering?"

Quentin looked amused. "That would be the million-dollar question, wouldn't it?" he quipped. "God knows why. Maybe he's a glutton for punishment."

Allison gave him a nonplussed look.

In response, Quent just looked at her consideringly. "Why don't you ask him?" he suggested finally.

"If I wanted to do that, I wouldn't have asked you, would I?" she returned tartly.

Quentin grinned. "Chicken."

She tossed her hair. "I don't know what you're talking about."

"Don't you?" Quentin replied as he headed back toward the door. "I'll be outside trying to pry the baby out of Mom's arms so I can get him into his car seat."

Soon after, Liz and Quentin departed the party, but not before Liz leaned in to whisper in her ear as they said goodbye, "Everything will be okay. You'll see."

On the drive back to Boston with Connor, Quentin's words sounded in Allison's head. *Why don't you ask him?*

Ten

Memorial Day. She should have been out playing with the rest of the world. Instead, she was in her kitchen, pretending to be doing…things.

The truth was, she was in the doldrums.

Connor was upstairs packing…despite the fact that so much remained unresolved between them. Despite the fact that she didn't want him to go.

A few weeks ago she would have said the idea was preposterous. But, a few weeks ago they hadn't been thrown together in the same house…they hadn't had wild and passionate sex…she hadn't fallen in love with him. He'd sneaked into her heart—if he'd ever left.

The fact that he'd refused to be paid to protect her

gave her some small measure of hope. There would have been a time when she'd have seen his volunteering as further evidence that Connor was just as overprotective as her family. But given what she knew of him now, she thought it was just another way for him to show he cared.

Connor protected those he cared about. It went to the core of what he was. It went back to being the son of a police officer killed in the line of duty, back to funding community projects in his old neighborhood.

Of course, the fact that he viewed the Whittakers as a substitute family could explain a lot about why he'd volunteered his services. He could simply have been doing her family a favor.

Yet, there was a part of her that refused to believe that was the whole explanation—at least, she hoped there was more to it. Because he hadn't only volunteered his company's services. Rather, he had insisted on protecting her himself when he could have delegated the task to someone on his staff, which would surely have been the logical thing to do since he probably had enough on his hands running his company.

When she'd thought Quentin was paying Connor for his services, she'd just assumed that her brother had insisted Connor take a personal hand in the matter. Instead, it had been Connor who had insisted. She liked to think it was because he cared about her, desired her…and more.

Quentin's question sounded in her head again. *Why don't you ask him?*

At a thump overhead, she looked up at the ceiling. Connor was up there packing and she was down here feeling all nervous and jittery. Butterflies fluttered in her stomach at the thought of the conversation she should be having with him, but inexplicable shyness made the task seem daunting.

Annoyed with herself, she threw down the dish towel she'd been absentmindedly using to wipe the kitchen counter.

As she went up, she thought about what she could say to him. *It's suddenly occurred to me that I love you? Our relationship may be a mistake, but it's a mistake I want to spend the rest of my life making?*

Maybe she should just start with, don't go. *Don't go. Please don't go.*

She walked along the upstairs hallway and stopped at the open doorway to the spare bedroom. Connor was tossing some jeans into a suitcase. Her heart wrenched.

He looked tough and forbidding. And pulse-flutteringly gorgeous. In a pale blue T-shirt and jeans, he projected a casual sexiness.

He looked up and, when he saw her standing in the doorway, he paused for a second, folded T-shirts in hand, before resuming his packing. "If you've come to do a victory dance at seeing the back of me, you're a little early. I won't be ready to walk out the door for a while yet."

She rubbed sweaty palms on the cargo pants she was wearing and walked into the room. "That's not why I'm here."

"Really?" He stopped packing and looked up at her. "Then why are you here, petunia?"

She bit her lip and then folded her hands together in front of her. "To say thank you. And to apologize."

He raised an eyebrow. "Thank you for what?"

"For helping me." She took a deep breath. "For capturing Kendall." *For defending me to my family. For making me love you.*

"And what's the apology for?"

"For giving you a hard time along the way."

"That's the second apology I've gotten from you in two weeks, princess." His lips curled into a sardonic smile. "Must be a record."

Despite her best intentions, she found herself becoming irritated by his taunting tone. And, frankly, it was easier to deal with him behind the shield of her annoyance. *Coward.* "What about the apology you owe me?" she demanded. "I haven't heard any apology cross your lips, Rafferty."

He sighed. "Okay, I'm going to play along here. Apology for what? Sleeping with you?"

Her lips tightened. "You purposely misled me

about your security services. Quentin didn't hire you. You volunteered."

He folded his arms and nodded. "All right, I admit I'm guilty of doing that. I apologize. Is that all you came here to say?"

"Why?" she asked.

"Why what?"

"Why did you volunteer?"

He regarded her for a second before answering, his face inscrutable. "Just following through on what I told Quentin I'd do, which was beefing up your security."

"No, I mean, why did you volunteer when Quentin could well have afforded to hire you? And why did you show up when you could have sent any number of the experts that Rafferty Security has on its payroll? Why did you insist on staying when you had no obligation to?" There, she'd gotten it out.

He unfolded his arms. "I think you know the answer to those questions," he said softly.

Her chin came up. "No, I don't. Why don't you enlighten me?"

"Have any theories suggested themselves?"

A quiver started in the pit of her stomach as he came closer. "You were doing a favor for a friend you consider to be practically family?"

He nodded, seeming to mull it over. "That would be a theory. Do you believe it?"

"Is it true?" she countered.

"No."

She backed up, but he kept on coming.

"I wouldn't say that was my major motivation, much as I like your family."

She skirted the side of the bed and found herself with her back to the wall. "You must not like them that much then," she said breathlessly.

He braced an arm against the wall near her head and caressed her cheek with the knuckles of his other hand. "Maybe I like you more."

Her heart plummeted. Like, not love.

She shoved at his chest and started to stalk past him, but he grabbed her arm and whirled her around. She felt the wall at her back seconds before his lips came down on hers.

It was the way it always was between them. A heavy dose of wanting and need shot through her. Her sense of the world around them dulled even as she became sensitized to his every touch…his lips molding hers…his body pressing against her.

She broke his hold on her to twine her arms around his neck, kissing him back with all the ardor she had kept pent up inside her.

As soon as he felt her willing response, he groaned and took the kiss deeper. His hands moved restlessly up and down her sides before one shimmied down her leg and then snaked around to cup her bottom and bring her flush up against him, letting her feel his erection.

Finally, he tore his mouth from hers and they broke apart. They were both breathing heavily. He looked as if he still had half a mind to take up where they had just left off, which was, she realized, not far from how she was feeling.

He spoke first. "You are hands-down the most frustrating woman I've ever known, petunia."

"Same goes," she parried.

And then his face was devoid of its usual sardonically amused expression, and what she read there made her breath catch in her throat. "Are you going to make me say it, princess?" He paused, holding her gaze so that she couldn't look away. "The reason I volunteered is that the thought of anything happening to you tore me up inside. I wanted to rip to shreds the bastard who was terrorizing you."

"Connor—"

"No, let me finish," he said fiercely. "I may never be as polished as the guys down at the country club, but I have plenty of money these days. You'd have trouble spending all of it even if you tried."

She nodded. A giddy happiness was growing and spreading within her. Not about the money, but about the fact that he was laying his soul bare.

"More importantly, we have tons of chemistry between us. The kind of chemistry that a lot of people spend a lifetime looking for and don't find."

She nodded again, her heart melting.

"And you sure as hell aren't going to find a man who loves you more than I do. Because it isn't possible. I'm so in love with you I ache with it."

He loved her. The confession was blunt and to the point—just like Connor—and she couldn't ask for anything more. Unexpected tears welled up in her eyes.

He gave her another fierce look. "So, get used it, petunia. You're under this tycoon's protection for the duration."

"May I say something?" she asked almost meekly, her smile tremulous.

"Only if it's what I'm waiting to hear. Are you ready to say the words, petunia? Because if you're not—" he looked down and gave her a slow, heated perusal "—I can be very convincing."

"Darn it, Rafferty," she said, blinking rapidly. "You're going to make me cry."

He caught a tear with the pad of his thumb. "Tears over me?" he said softly.

"Yes," she said, then sniffed and blinked. "You are the most irritating and annoyingly smug man I've ever met and I love you. Madly and passionately."

He grinned, genuine happiness suffusing his face. "I'd say mad and passionate sort of sums up our relationship."

"We'll never be dull," she agreed.

"I can't believe you were going to let me walk out that door today."

"I can't believe you were planning to walk out," she countered.

He gave her a lopsided grin. "Even if I had, I'd already formulated a backup plan."

"Oh?" she inquired. "And what would that be?"

"To woo you and make such a pest of myself that you'd realize we were destined to be together."

"I realized that long ago," she said wryly.

He looked surprised. "Do tell."

Since they were being completely honest, she figured she owed him the truth. "I had the teenage crush on you to end all teenage crushes."

He chuckled. "Now *that* I find hard to believe."

"Believe it," she said firmly. "Why do you think I was in that bar that night? Why do you think it was so humiliating for me to have you of all people turn me in to my parents?"

"You were there because you thought I'd be there?" he asked, astonishment showing on his face.

She nodded. "I figured if I acted grown up, you'd think I was. Instead, you hauled me home as if I were a sack of potatoes."

He shook his head. "If I'd known you were there for me, I'm not sure I could have resisted you up to now."

Now it was her turn to look disbelieving. "I thought you did a good job of acting as if I were completely resistible."

"*Acting* would be the operative word there," he

said dryly. "Over the years, it became easy to treat you as if you were just a spoiled little rich girl. It meant I didn't have to analyze my feelings too closely."

"You said something in the kitchen after I had turned the water nozzle on you—"

He smiled. "Yeah, how can I forget?"

"You referred to 'what's always been between us.' I thought you knew about my teenage crush."

"No." He shook his head. "I meant the electricity that practically crackles between us whenever we're in the same room."

She reached out to caress his jaw, tracing the crescent-shaped scar on his chin. "Why didn't you ever say anything?"

He sighed but his eyes remained intense on hers. "You were the younger sister of my old college buddy. The precious gem of a socially prominent family. The daughter of people who've treated me like a son." He paused. "There's a trust there that you don't betray."

"Sometimes I wish they wouldn't think of me as quite so precious," she grumbled. Yet, she had to respect Connor's code of honor. It was part of why she loved him, she realized.

"I know, petunia." He turned his head and kissed her palm. "But it's only because they care."

"I lumped you in the same category with them,

you know. Then I realized that what I thought of as high-handed overprotectiveness was just a way for you to show you cared."

"Oh, I cared all right." He gave her a quick kiss on the lips. "But how did you come to that realization?"

"It was the night in the Berkshires. When you were talking about your father and then going back into your old neighborhood to try to make peoples' lives safer. I realized that's the way you showed you cared. By protecting the people and things you loved."

He smiled but shook his head. "Before you give me too much credit, I did use some heavy-handed techniques where you were concerned."

"You don't say?" she teased. "You mean, like getting the key to my house from Quentin? And moving right in when I told you to get lost?"

He looked contrite. "Yeah, that. In my defense, I'll say that it was only because I was scared out of my mind that something might happen to you." He added, "But, you were right that I wasn't giving you the credit you deserved. If you want to continue at the DA's Office—"

She put her finger on his lips. "Shh." She knew how hard this was for him. Having lost his father, it would be tough to see someone else he loved in harm's way. "You taught me not to be so lackadaisical about my safety and you were right. I thought I'd done a fairly good job by taking self-defense classes. The truth was I was a bit cavalier. I'd been raised in a tight-knit family in a nice, quiet community and nothing terrible had ever happened to me. Certainly nothing as bad as having a parent shot and killed by a burglar."

His shoulders relaxed. It was clear he was glad she understood that part of his nature.

"As for the DA's Office, I'm going to take it one day at a time. Now that Kendall's been caught, the immediate threat is gone. I don't know how long I'll stick to the prosecutor's job," she admitted, "but I know that, for now, that's where I want to be."

He nodded. "I can't promise I'll always succeed, but I'll try hard to keep my protective instincts in check."

She smiled at him, tears threatening again. "That's all I ask." She added, "And, by the way, what was it that persuaded you to take our relationship to the next level, when, as you said, you were worried about betraying my family's trust?"

"The fact that someone was threatening you," he said simply. "When I realized something might happen to you, I knew I'd kick myself if I didn't at least try to explore what was between us."

He rubbed her upper arms with the palms of his hands. "Ultimately though, I'm not sure the decision was that conscious. I knew moving in with you was going to test my resolve to keep my hands off you, and I was right. Once I moved in, one thing led to another…."

"Because we hit sparks off each other."

"Exactly."

"Well, I just want to set the record straight. I never thought you were beneath me. Like you, I had my defensive mechanisms. To the extent you dismissed me as a spoiled, rich princess, I was going to try to live up to the image in the most obnoxious way possible."

"By calling us a mistake, for instance?" he asked, eyebrows raised.

She looked at him, surprised. "Is that what you thought I meant?"

He shrugged. "Seemed logical."

She shook her head. "What I actually meant was that, if you still thought of me as little better than an impetuous teenager, then I didn't think we had the makings of a relationship based on mutual trust and respect."

He looked deeply into her eyes. "You've got my trust and respect. And my love. Don't ever doubt it." He took her hand then and led her to the bed. He watched with hot eyes as she kicked off her sandals and shimmied out of her cargo pants, then pulled her white T-shirt over her head, so that she was clad only in her bra and panties.

"Aren't you going to take off anything?" she teased.

"Mmm," he responded as he reached out to caress her shoulders, a glint of amusement lighting his eyes. "Since you only have on a bra and panties, there isn't much to choose from."

Allison laughed. "Connor, that's not what I meant—"

"But I think I'll go with the bra," he continued smoothly before undoing the front clasp of her bra with a flick of the fingers. As she spilled out of the loosened cups, his eyes darkened with desire.

Letting the bra slide down her arms and drop to the floor, she said breathlessly, "Now your turn."

He unsnapped his jeans and lowered the zipper, which made a rasping sound as it opened. She helped him slide his boxers and jeans down his hips as he kicked off his shoes and then tugged his shirt over his head.

Rising back up from helping him out of his jeans, she reached out and stroked his arousal.

He sucked in a breath. "Ah, petunia."

"Love me," she said, her voice husky.

Bending toward the bed, he made a sweeping motion with his arm, sending his bag and clothes sliding off the blanket and onto the floor. Then he picked her up as easily as if she were nothing more than a bit of fluff and deposited her on the bed before coming down beside her.

His mouth moved to her breast, sending spasms

of pleasure through her, before moving to her other breast and doing the same. Finally, when she thought she couldn't stand it any longer, he raised his head for a long, slow, drugging kiss.

His hands caressed her, finding her pleasure points, making her moan. "Connor—"

"Yes," he said gruffly, distracted by running kisses down the side of her neck.

She caressed his back, running her hands over his sinewy muscles, feeling them flex under her fingers. The anticipation was nearly too much as he built a response from her. "Please."

He reached down between their bodies and touched her. His breath came harshly, his desire held in check, until she moaned, arched, and pulled him to her.

He put on some protection then and positioned himself, giving her a hard kiss before sliding into her with a groan.

"Oh, Connor."

They began to move together, slowly at first and then faster, while her world dimmed to just the two of them.

When they climaxed simultaneously, her world exploded in spasms of sensation followed by a feeling of completeness and contentment that was total and encompassing.

Afterward, she snuggled close to him.

"You are a wonder," he growled.

She laughed.

"Allison," he said.

"Yes?"

"Will you marry me?"

She raised her head and looked at him. "You mean, will I spend the rest of my life arguing with you? Disagreeing with your judgment? And, in general, being a thorn in your side?" she asked.

He arched a brow. "Yeah, that sounds about right."

She smiled. She was sure her face was glowing with happiness. "Yes, I will."

Epilogue
_____

"**H**ow the haughty have fallen," Noah Whittaker said with a grin.

Allison tossed her hair over her shoulder and looked up from the bridal magazine she was perusing. Her brothers and sister-in-law had stopped by the townhouse for some food and conversation on a lazy Sunday afternoon. Having just finished lunch, they were now sitting in the living room with baby Nicholas asleep in his carrier.

"Don't pay any attention to him, Allison," Liz advised. She shot Noah a reproving look. "Love is a beautiful thing."

Noah raised his glass in salute. "Right. A beautiful thing that hasn't happened to me," he said, his tone practically gleeful.

Allison narrowed her eyes. "Laugh while you can, copper top," she said using her old childhood moniker for Noah, whose reddish-brown hair was several shades lighter than that of any of his siblings.

After her successful matchmaking with Quentin and Liz, Allison had jokingly threatened to get Noah married off, too, partly because he pretended to be such a cynic. Instead, with no apparent effort on her brother's part, she herself would be the one walking down the aisle next. Noah was obviously relishing the fact that events had panned out the way they had, and he'd escaped the marital noose— for now.

Connor walked into the living room holding a couple of open beers, one of which he handed to Matt. "What's going on?"

As usual, Allison's heart swelled at the sight of him. It wasn't every woman who got the chance to marry the star of her teenage dreams. "Noah is just gloating over the fact that I'm going to walk down the aisle before he does."

"Well, it's not as if he didn't try to give matters a helping hand," Connor said as he came to sit on the couch next to her, giving her a lecherous look when no one else could see.

She felt herself blush even as she shot him a reproving look. "What do you mean?" she asked distractedly.

"Er, Connor—" Noah said.

Out of the corner of her eye, she saw Noah make a slashing motion across his throat while amusement lit Quentin's face.

"Yes, what do you mean, Connor?" Liz piped up, shooting Noah a look of curiosity.

"Well, let's just say Noah and I had an interesting conversation at the Memorial Day barbecue. Something along the lines of—"

Noah groaned and let his head fall back against his leather chair.

"—doing your family a favor by marrying you," Connor finished.

Liz gasped while Allison let her mouth open in surprise.

Still staring at the ceiling, Noah asked, "Whatever happened to the concept of brotherhood? Men sticking together?"

"Out the window once you're going to gloat about it," Connor replied, amusement coloring his voice. "Besides, pal, your plan to get Allison hitched meant I'd be getting hitched, too. There had to be a payback for that."

"Noah, how could you?" Allison asked, then added, answering herself, "Never mind. That was a rhetorical question. I've known you for thirty years. I think I know exactly how you could."

Quentin laughed. "You've gotten a dose of your own matchmaking medicine, Ally. How does it feel?"

"The difference is that I knew you and Liz were meant for each other," Allison sniffed.

Quentin and Noah exchanged looks, but it was Matt who spoke. "I hate to tell you, sis, but you and Connor had lovebirds written all over you lately. Bickering lovebirds, but lovebirds nevertheless."

Allison flushed. They'd been that transparent?

"Well, that I'll agree with," said Liz.

"And let's not talk about that case of puppy love that you used to have," Noah teased.

Allison ignored Noah's teasing and turned to Connor, pasting a look of mock offense on her face. "And, you, what do you mean there had to be a payback for trying to get you married?"

Connor raised his arm from the back of the couch and stroked her hair. "Just that, I knew that if I told you about Noah's little suggestion, petunia, you and Liz would double your efforts to get him married so he can be almost as blissfully happy as I am."

Noah guffawed and Quentin chuckled.

Matt raised a brow. "Laying it on thick, aren't you Rafferty?"

"I'd say that he's already developed the right attitude for marriage," Quentin disagreed.

Liz nodded. "He's good." She turned to Noah. "You, on the other hand, will wise up soon, I hope."

Noah gave a mock shudder. "Yeah, well, if the gossip columns are to be believed, I'm doing a good job of dating every woman under the sun to find the right woman." He frowned. "There's this one columnist in particular who, I swear, seems to think I'm a cross between Casanova and Rudolph Valentino."

Allison laughed. "Love it."

"Anyway," Noah went on, "what's the problem? By his own admission, Connor is *blissfully* happy and I haven't seen you this cheery since—" he pretended to scratch his head "—uh, since—"

Allison tossed a pillow at him, but Noah ducked.

Yet, Noah was right.

She looked at Connor, knowing that love was written as plainly on her face as it was on his. "You know, brother dear, you may be joking but you also happen to be right in this case. I don't think I've ever been this happy."

As Connor closed in for a kiss, Allison sighed and let her eyes flutter shut. Yes, love was a beautiful thing. A beautiful thing that had finally happened to her.

* * * * *

COMING NEXT MONTH

#1645 JUST A TASTE—Bronwyn Jameson
Dynasties: The Ashtons
When Jillian Ashton's arrogant husband died, it wasn't long before she found a man who treated her right—*really* right. Problem was, Seth—a tall, dark and handsome hunk—was her late husband's brother. She'd planned on just a taste of his tender touch, but was left wanting more....

#1646 DOUBLE IDENTITY—Annette Broadrick
The Crenshaws of Texas
Undercover agent Jude Crenshaw only meant to attract Carina Patterson for the sake of cracking a case against her brothers. But when close quarters turned his business into their pleasure, Jude could only hope his double identity wouldn't turn their new union into two broken hearts.

#1647 RULES OF ATTRACTION—Susan Crosby
Behind Closed Doors
P.I. Quinn Gerard was following a suspected accomplice—or so he thought. When the sexy bombshell turned out to be her twin sister, Claire, Quinn no longer had to watch her every move. But he couldn't seem to take his eyes off her! Could Quinn convince Claire to bend the rules and give in to their mutual attraction?

#1648 WHEN THE EARTH MOVES—Roxanne St. Claire
After Jo Ellen Tremaine's best friend died during an earthquake, she was determined to adopt her friend's baby girl. But first she needed the permission of the girl's stunningly sexy uncle—big-shot attorney Cameron McGrath. Cameron always had a weakness for wildly attractive women, but neither was prepared for the aftershocks of this seismic shift....

#1649 BEYOND BUSINESS—Rochelle Alers
The Blackstones of Virginia
Blackstone Farms owner Sheldon Blackstone couldn't help but be enraptured by his newly hired assistant, Renee Williams. Little did he know she was pregnant with her ex's baby. Renee was totally taken by this older man, but could she convince him to make her—and her child—his forever?

#1650 SLEEPING ARRANGEMENTS—Amy Jo Cousins
The terms of the will were clear: in order to gain her inheritance Addy Tyler needed to be married. Enter the one man she never dreamed would become her groom of convenience—Spencer Reed. Their marriage was supposed to be hands-off, but their sleeping arrangements changed everything!

SDCNM0305

PRIMROSE PEACOCK

Line illustrations by Rosemary Godsell

Discovering
Old Buttons

SHIRE PUBLICATIONS LTD

Contents

ACKNOWLEDGEMENTS

The author acknowledges with thanks the help received from the following: Madelaine Ginsberg (Victoria and Albert Museum); Rosemary Godsell; Richard Jeffreys (Watts Gallery); Monica Jones; the late Peggy Sweeny (Denver, Colorado); Deidre White (City of Birmingham Museum); Martock Mobile Library.

Unless individually acknowledged in brackets all buttons illustrated in line are from the author's collection.

Photographs are acknowledged as follows: Leicester Museum, plate 1; Crown copyright, Victoria and Albert Museum, plates 2, 3; City of Birmingham Museum, plates 4, 5, 6, 9, 10, 16; Mr F. Schmitte, plates 14, 15; Mr S. Godsell, plate 17; Mr D. Temperley, plate 18 (City of Birmingham Museum print).

Printed in Great Britain by C. I. Thomas & Sons (Haverfordwest) Ltd.

Introduction

Buttons have been widely used as both fasteners and decoration since the sixth century AD. Originating with the introduction of fitted clothing in the Middle East, they have followed fashions in both dress and upholstery ever since. There are therefore countries and periods when because of current fashion or even prevailing tax laws few buttons originate. In contrast, during the eighteenth and nineteenth centuries buttons for first male and later female costume achieved great prominence.

Uniform buttons, outside the scope of this book, originate wherever military activity existed during the periods when fitted clothes were used. During the last two hundred years buttons have been widely used on civilian uniforms ranging from those of noble dignitaries to the humble 'buttons'.

In the USA decorative buttons have been avidly collected since the 1930s. There the hobby vaguely resembles philately in organisation, with national and regional button societies and publications. As a result of this interest many collector's terms have been coined. Some of these are explained in the glossary; others are given in brackets in the text. In Britain interest in old buttons as collector's objects is more recent, but growing.

In Britain buttons are measured in lines. Forty lines equal one inch. It is not possible in a work of this size to describe every type of button ever made, as some manufactories were small, others failed or were very localised. Also, often for reasons of either sentiment or eccentricity, a few odd buttons have occasionally been made from some quite extraordinary or rare substances!

1. The history of buttons

Early buttons

Although buttons have been known to date from as early as the sixth century AD, when fitted clothing was introduced in the Middle East, the average collector is unlikely to see either buttons or portrayals of them dating before the fourteenth century. Buttons made from small pieces of cloth sewn into a tight knob were among fragments of clothing found when the site of the Royal Wardrobe in the Blackfriars Bridge area of London was excavated in 1972. They have been dated to the mid fourteenth century. Buttons are also depicted on effigies of this period, including that of Walter de Helyan in Much Marcle church near Hereford, in Westminster Abbey and Reepham church, Norfolk. Contemporary writers refer to gilt and silver gilt buttons being ordered for royalty and nobility of the day.

In Tudor times costume in Britain and Europe had become elaborate and was initially colourful and frequently decorated with numerous buttons made from precious metals and gemstones. There is now one such example in a private collection in the midlands. Many such buttons were later melted down and used either to make jewellery or to pay the debts of their owners. Later, owing to Spanish influence, sombre colours were worn but portraits of the time show numerous buttons, generally made from metals, on male costume. The clothes of working people were simple and adorned with buttons made from leather or plain metal discs with a soldered wire shank. They are very difficult to date precisely.

The seventeenth century saw many changes in costume, notably the use of ribbons and lacing, particularly in female clothing, but during this period the frock coat and vest or waistcoat were introduced for men. Both garments were decorated with numerous buttons. Many of these, now called passementerie, were made from braids, threads and fabrics drawn over moulds and matching the garment material. Beads and sequins were used for decoration. Leather, wood, metals and bones were also used.

Eighteenth-century European buttons

Many of the world's finest buttons were made in Europe, including Russia, during this period. In an era of fine craftsmanship, easy access to materials of intrinsic value and an abundance of affluent customers the button makers excelled themselves. Many of them were goldsmiths or silversmiths in their own right or very closely associated with the jewellery trade. It was natural for the elegant man requiring ornamentation for his elaborate clothing to ask his jeweller for advice. The jeweller in turn might commission an artist or craftsman to assist him. Many outstanding sets of buttons were specifically commissioned in this way and were worn on men's coats, breeches and waistcoats more for ornamentation than as fasteners. Women's clothing, although elaborate with layers of billowing skirts, did not require many decorative buttons.

Many eighteenth-century buttons are about 10p (50 cent) size and were constructed by mounting a painting or carving under glass within a metal shell with a loop shank. Others were enamelled, set with jewels, engraved on precious metals or made from hand-painted porcelain. Carved shell was often inlaid with paste or jewels and other popular varieties included marcasite, inlaid hardstone known as petro dura and a continuation of passementerie types. The D'Allemagne Collection of Paris, now in New Jersey, and the Rothschild Collection, now at Waddesdon Manor, Buckinghamshire, illustrate these techniques and others.

As this type of button was avidly collected by Americans during the immediate post-war period they are now scarce outside established collections, but some have been converted to brooches and these occur fairly frequently in Britain although they have lost their value as buttons.

Eighteenth-century British buttons

The Luckock Collection now in Birmingham Museum represents much of the best of British button making of the period. This collection was assembled by James Luckock, a Birmingham jeweller, between 1844 and 1849 and includes Wedgwood jasper medallions mounted as buttons, carved pearls, engraved silver and some of the under-glass techniques. It was during this period that the metal button industry grew and flourished in England owing to a prohibition on cloth-covered buttons and export orders received from America and the colonies. Established British companies of the period, including some primarily engaged in making uniform buttons, are Firmin and Sons Ltd (1667), Hammond Turner and Sons Ltd (1717), J. & R. Gaunt Ltd and Jennens and Co. Several Birmingham inhabitants, including John Smith, William Collins and William Bell, took out patents for new methods of decorating and finishing metal buttons between 1770 and 1779. At this time the beginnings of the horn and shell button businesses were taking place in the midlands. The manufacture of the large brass and copper buttons now known in America as colonials was also based on Birmingham and included at least one type of 'Washington Inaugural' — a special button worn by delegates to the 1789 and 1793 inaugurations and made by Gaunt's. Matthew Boulton played a prominent part in the production of steel mounts for fine buttons.

In Dorset and Staffordshire there were flourishing peasant industries concerned with the making of thread buttons, either using small pieces of bone or horn as moulds, or working threads cartwheel fashion on wire rings obtained from Birmingham. There may too have been some small-scale glass button making in areas connected with the glass trade, but precise evidence is hard to find and human memory often faulty on provenance.

Eighteenth-century American buttons

Before independence (1776) and for the next three decades the majority of buttons used in America were imported, chiefly from Britain, Holland and France. The rapid growth of the American industry was a nineteenth-century phenomenon. However, as early as 1763 the inventory of John Jennings's shop at Norwalk, Connecticut, included both silver and stone buttons (probably stonewear) and in 1767 reference can be found to one Joseph Hopkins of Waterbury, Connecticut, as a producer of silver buttons. In the same state Samuel Yale of Meriden made pewter buttons from 1790 and a number of small concerns in the New Haven area began to make metal buttons at about this time. Connecticut later became the centre of the industry.

Some of the first American-produced buttons were those made by Caspar Wister, a young German immigrant to Philadelphia, who started hollow-cast brass button making in the 1720s. His products, guaranteed for seven years, became internationally famous and attracted imitators, including Henry Wrightman of New York City. Wister's son Richard continued with the business but a grandson became a doctor and is now remembered by the shrub wisteria, named in his memory. In 1770 Benjamin Randolph of Philadelphia advertised various hardwood buttons and from 1789 Phineas Pratt, who owned an ivory workshop in Ivorytown, Connecticut, produced buttons and studs as a sideline to his main business of making piano keys. This business had begun with the use of tusks brought from Africa as marine ballast and discarded on arrival in America.

Nineteenth-century European buttons

During this period European manufactories, especially in France, lost much of their eighteenth-century pre-eminence and were in some cases slow to mechanise. Good-quality buttons were, however, constantly produced by an industry largely based in Paris, with Trelon, Weldon and Weil and Albert Parent and Co. being leading manufacturers. Once the secrets of the pressed clay process had been obtained from Britain, Bapertrosses of Braire cornered this market and did an enormous export business, particularly with America.

Most other European countries had growing button industries, but it was not until they began to export widely towards the end of the century that their products became known to the world at large. Except in the Vienna area, much of the trade was fragmented and loosely organised, often being a very badly paid peasant industry. Some countries such as Holland, Scandinavia, Spain and Portugal, while making good buttons for their national costumes and home markets, appear seldom to have exported them other than to their colonies.

The last twenty years of the nineteenth century saw an enormous increase in button production, due to current trends in fashion, and this continued into the early twentieth century. As it is almost impossible to distinguish a button made in 1880 from a similar one made in 1912 they are discussed under the heading *Edwardian buttons*.

Nineteenth-century British buttons

In the early years of the century the British button industry expanded rapidly. Following a general mechanisation in the middle years and resulting mass production it achieved a prominent position in the world.

Initially male clothing was dark with gilt buttons and ladies' garments, being neo-classical, did not require buttons, but by 1875, following the rise and fall of the crinoline, men were wearing cloth-covered or plain buttons of sombre hues, but ladies' clothing was smothered in all kinds of buttons and trims. This fashion continued until the First World War.

Some of the most significant developments in British button making were the invention of the florentine button in 1801, the cloth or flexible shank in 1825, Aston's patent button-making machine for linen-covered buttons, invented in 1841 and causing the demise of the thread button industry, and the Prosser pressed clay process. Later the importation of buffalo horn and corozo or dum nuts resulted in mass reorganisation after a period of slump and the subsequent production of natural horn and vegetable ivory buttons. The most profitable branches of the industry were initially gilt metal buttons, followed by shell. Both trades were based in Birmingham. Because of Britain's position as head of an ever growing empire, her close ties with America and the abilities of her people to organise, British buttons became world-famous and have since been found wherever the white man went.

Nineteenth-century American buttons

The nineteenth century was also a great growth period for the American button industry. During the first part of the century efforts were concentrated on learning and perfecting manufacturing techniques from Britain and Europe in addition to the continuance and development of eighteenth-century processes. Some fine metal buttons, in particular, were made before the Civil War, together with some other types exclusive to America. The Civil War (1861-5) disrupted production and caused demand to exceed home-based capabilities, resulting in British firms making uniform buttons for American armies. Later the American industry, aided by an influx of European immigrants, expanded rapidly and as a result of experimentation produced hard rubber, celluloid and various composition buttons which were the forerunners of modern synthetic materials.

Before 1860 America did not export buttons and even after that date imports exceeded exports, vast numbers being obtained from Europe and Britain by the end of the century. The button industry was not surprisingly based on the east coast, with groups of factories in Connecticut, Massachusetts and Pennsylvania, but once fresh-water shell had been discovered as a raw material factories sprang up along the banks of the Mississippi. Owing to collector interest the history of the American button industry has now been well documented in books and magazines published there.

Edwardian buttons

The last two decades of the nineteenth century and the period up to the First World War, often loosely referred to as the Edwardian period, represent the peak of the decorative button manufactory and a significant attempt was made to reproduce eighteenth-century beauty with a partial revival of techniques previously discarded. Enamel and porcelain buttons, not generally made during the early nineteenth century, are typical of the latter trend and the mass production of the two-piece and three-piece fancy metals of the former. During this period ladies' clothing was not only undergoing changes in style, but the invention of paper patterns and home sewing machines resulted in a boom in the haberdashery business. Buttons were used not merely as fasteners, but also to decorate women's and children's clothing.

The industrial revolution and its accompanying traumas were over by 1880 so that manufacturers equipped with then modern machinery and plentiful cheap labour in Britain, Europe and America were able to produce an amazing diversity of styles for incredibly low prices. This was also a period of experimentation, and combinations of metals and of metal with other materials were widely used. In America more than Britain there was a great interest in buttons depicting current show-business personalities, historical incidents, national monuments and the like, but generally fewer art nouveau design buttons were made there than in France or Britain. The American button makers did not try to revive eighteenth-century styles as the French and Belgians did. Several Paris and Brussels companies produced sets of champleve and painted enamel buttons; others made porcelain imitations of Sevres to match parasol handles or copied under-glass techniques in cheap materials. Studs and hatpin heads were made to match.

Steel made a brief comeback and glass was used to imitate the marcasite and jewelled buttons of an earlier era. The art nouveau silver button was of British origin, but similar styles in brass and glass came from several European countries. This was the age of the grand-style tourist with accompanying buying habits. As a result the Italians made glass paperweight-style buttons, the Japanese Satsumas, the Chinese enamels and hardstone and various other countries from Persia to Russia produced buttons quite dissimilar to anything worn on native dress, but easily carried away by the foreign visitor. The clothing of the heathen by Victorian missionaries also assisted the button trade. Utilitarian buttons were mass-produced in vegetable ivory, shell, linen and various substances loosely called composition.

Between the world wars

During the 1920s few decorative buttons were produced as women's fashions did not require them. Covered fabric and glass buttons were used on children's clothes and the rubber liberty bodice button was Nanny's *bete noire*. A range of fancy (sometimes vulgar) buttons was made for men's waistcoats using clear celluloid or glass over small pictures set in a metal mount. Exotic varieties were made for evening dress until ousted by the double-breasted rig. The change in women's clothes to longer and more feminine styles resulted in greater scope for button makers, with enormous buttons in wood or casein having a vogue. Designs now known as art deco appeared on glass, wood, metal and covered fabric buttons. Vegetable ivory was gradually going out of favour. Bone, steel and hardstone buttons became obsolete. To judge by old shop stock of the period, it appears that Britain imported more buttons than she made. Painted metals, vegetable ivory, glass and covered buttons on European cards are found in quantity.

In America the growing population and the influx of European refugees and immigrants resulted in earlier types of button continuing. Fresh-water mollusc shells from American rivers were used from 1890 until after the Second World War. There was also mass importation of pressed clay small china buttons from France and Bohemia, and some trade with Japan and other Asian countries. Generally, however, the day of the fine button was over and little of either great intrinsic value or superb craftsmanship has been made since the First World War.

Modern buttons

The years immediately succeeding the Second World War were difficult ones for British and European manufacturers because of loss of premises and shortage of labour or materials, and they had to make do with what they could find. Therefore it is not surprising that some rather strange products came on the market, including buttons made from plaster of paris, plastic-covered or plain wire, pulped paper, hardboard, cork, scrap metal, perspex and rabbit fur. Such may be interesting to the social historian but are hardly collector's items.

American factories were less affected by the war, although many made uniform buttons, and they quickly built up production but were the first to feel the impact of the zip fastener. During the 1950s and the 1960s changes in fashion styles, the development of modern synthetic materials, the zip and the spin drier resulted in widespread discontinuation of many button types in Britain and America. Shell and glass went first, followed gradually by some metals, although a plastic-coated metal became popular, as did natural horn in conjunction with leather clothing. Wooden buttons were made for heavy knitwear. On the Continent, however, Austria produced a huge range of quite attractive metal buttons and Czechoslovakia and West Germany recommenced glass button making, exporting widely, particularly to America, until very recently. Vegetable ivory was used in Spain and Italy for some years but is obsolete now.

Recently there have been limited attempts to meet the public demand for attractive buttons in Britain. A London sports-trophy manufacturer made a range of champleve enamels for a short period. Two small concerns made decorated glass buttons sold in Harrods in 1973 and some metal restrikes have been produced by old established companies. A limited number of shell buttons are still imported for high-class shirts; others with stuck plastic shanks have been used on woollen garments, but generally the British manufacturing industry is resistant to all suggestions as to how it might depart from the mass-produced synthetic disc. Many small firms bombed during the war never reopened and some larger companies have merged.

In America many older firms closed after the war when they had to decide whether to change to synthetic materials or fall behind. However button making continues there, assisted by importation, especially from south-east Asia. There are also a few firms which specialise in importing unusual buttons for the garment trade. JHB Imports of Denver, Colorado, is one of them. The making of small numbers of 'studio' buttons for collectors can hardly be classed as manufacturing, being generally small-scale and transitory, but the Japanese have recently made reproduction satsuma pottery and enamel buttons for export to America.

Future trends are hard to predict and will be entirely the result of current fashion demands, but the button, even if purely utilitarian, is unlikely to become obsolete yet awhile.

Fig. 1. METAL BUTTONS
1. Modern aluminium; probably Czechoslovakian. 2. Alloy pictorial button; c. 1910. 3. Alloy brace (suspender) button; early twentieth century. 4. French brass, die-stamped; c. 1890. 5. British brass sporting button; c. 1820. 6 and 7. Two-piece pressed brass buttons; early twentieth century. 8. Bronzed alloy with a design known as Kate Greenaway (R.Godsell). 9 and 10. Bronze finished two-piece metal buttons; c. 1900. 11. Small buttons known as Austrian tinies; early twentieth century.

11

2. Metal buttons

More buttons have been made of metal than of any other substance, the majority being wholly or partly of brass. Even with the widespread use of synthetic substances, some of which are now used to make buttons superficially resembling metal, it is unlikely that metal button making will be discontinued for a long time.

Metal buttons or their component parts are made by one of two basic methods: casting — pouring molten metal into a prepared mould; or by cutting from sheet metal. They can be finished by numerous different processes and then either have sewing holes drilled or one of a variety of shank attached. Depending on the number of separate pieces used to make a metal button, it is referred to by collectors as a one-piece, two-piece or three-piece metal. Metals are widely used in conjunction with other materials.

Many American collectors assemble their metal and other buttons according to the decorative subject depicted on the face and for competitive purposes numerous classifications have evolved. These are not always relevant to manufacturing process, age or costume association. Thus a bicycle or inanimate button refers to one which by chance depicts a cycle or some inanimate object like a hat. Such buttons were not necessarily made for cycling clothes.

Alloy

Alloy is the term given to a mixture of two or more pure metals. Brass is an alloy of copper and zinc; pewter and bronze are also alloys. However, button collectors tend to use this term to describe metal buttons made from less well-known or unknown combinations. These are numerous.

Aluminium

There are two distinct types of aluminium button. At the end of the nineteenth century aluminium, then very expensive, was used by the Scoville Manufacturing Co. of Waterbury, Connecticut, to produce finely chased and stamped three-piece buttons with an intermediate of some other material. Such buttons were not made in Britain. Recently a few uniform buttons have been made from aluminium and a modern pressed type with a painted decoration has appeared. Aluminium is very light in weight and will not rust, but it is easily confused with alloys or tin (which rusts easily).

Brass

The earliest type of brass button dating from the seventeenth century was made by covering a wood or bone mould with thin sheet brass. Crossed catgut loops formed the shank. Solid cast brass buttons were widely made during the eighteenth century and

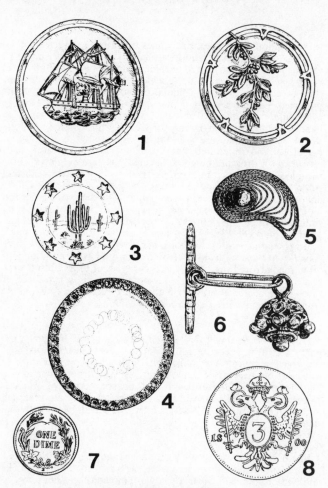

Fig. 2. METAL BUTTONS

1. Three-piece metal button (brass and alloy) depicting a nineteenth-century Atlantic packet; c. 1900. 2. Three-piece (brass on tin) decorative button; European, c. 1910. 3. Modern American Indian copper button from Arizona. 4. British eighteenth-century copper coat button; known as a colonial in America. 5. Stamped brass to simulate filigree; European, twentieth century. 6. Nineteenth-century filigree button; probably Dutch. 7. Button made from an American coin. 8. A three-kreuzer Austrian copper coin which has been Sheffield-plated and converted into a button; Francis II of Austria and other Hapsburg lands.

with variations ever since. Early ones had a cone-shaped knob on the back through which a hole was drilled, but later wire shanks of various patterns were brazed or soldered to the back. Rolling brass sheet was a Birmingham trade which the Americans took some time to acquire, so their colonial-period buttons were generally imported. Large brass and copper buttons sometimes referred to as *colonials* were made from sheet metal and then decorated by hand with punches, engraving tools or a lathe (engine turning). Worn by men, they are still fairly easily found in Britain; if neglected and separated from their shanks they are easily mistaken for dirty *old* pennies. Cleaned, they are delightful. Fine two-piece die-stamped buttons, particularly if portraying sporting subjects, were very popular during the early nineteenth century and were made by numerous companies. The dies were produced independently. Hipwood and Steeple was one Birmingham company which specialised in this work for both home and overseas markets. Eight differing designs were worn on a man's hunting coat according to choice and they are now referred to as *sporting buttons* to avoid confusion with hunt club buttons, also often made from brass. Later, cheaper types of brass button were made by pressing thin sheet and mounting it as a two-piece or three-piece button. Millions of uniform buttons were also made from this metal. See also *Copper* and *Gilt*.

Bronzed alloy

During the period 1875-1914 numerous metal buttons were made with a bronzed finish in order to prevent tarnish, rust and the need for repeated cleaning. Although often now attractive to collectors because of the range of interesting subjects depicted on their faces, these buttons were the cheap products of Austria, Germany, Bohemia and America in their day. They are plentiful in Britain and often have black-painted (japanned) backs and loop shanks.

Combinations

Metal combinations are legion and cannot be fully described here. Some of those most frequently seen are small half-inch (13 mm) buttons made in Austria and worn on ladies' clothes between 1880 and 1925, or later if stocks were available. Known as *Austrian tinies,* they have domed backs and loop shanks, with a wide variety of skilfully designed facial decoration. Some incorporate other materials such as celluloid or fabric. Originally they sold for as little as 1½d (1p or 2 cents) for half a dozen, which is amazing considering the work involved.

Coin

It is now illegal in both Britain and America to convert currency into buttons, but at one time buttons made from coins were given

14

to young American men reaching their majority. These were known as *freedom buttons*. Buttons made from European currencies occur in Britain, where several denominations of small coins have also been converted. However, the button is not necessarily as old as the coin date, particularly if made from Maundy money. Metal buttons made to resemble coins are relatively modern and often Austrian in origin, although the representation may be of a Greek or Roman coin. They have blank backs and no special merit.

Copper

Copper was used during the eighteenth century to make large buttons for men's clothing (see *Brass*) but fell into general disuse later. During the past forty years this metal has been used by primitive peoples and studio workers to make hand-wrought buttons for collectors and tourists. It is also a suitable base metal for enamel work.

Filigree

This name is given to any button made from either fine wire work or stamped metal to resemble it. True filigree is wire work. Silver wire buttons were made in India, Burma and adjacent countries as early tourist items. A rather heavier variety has been made for two hundred years in European countries, being usually ball-shaped and often linked in pairs or mounted with a link and bar. It is used in national costumes from Norway to Spain and there are many distinct patterns, some very localised (see *Foreign silver*). Brass wire work was briefly popular between the wars and simulated filigree has been produced spasmodically for a long time.

Gilt

At the beginning of the nineteenth century male fashions required finely gilded one-piece or two-piece brass buttons decorated with cut and chased designs. The process of making them was centred in Birmingham but was later learnt by American manufacturers. The buttons were dipped one or more times in a special amalgam containing gold. Collectors call these buttons *golden age*. They are a study in themselves and now well documented. They have great social and historical associations, being replaced by the florentine button in Britain, despite petitions to the king by their makers. Spurious ones were also the subject of a court case in their day. Generally, however, they were well made and frequently backstamped with legends such as *triple gilt*, *superfine*, *extra fine* or *Victoria*. Recently cheap tin-plated buttons have been advertised as gilts in auction catalogues, so collectors are warned!

Lead

Lead alone was seldom used to make buttons, although it is often one part of an alloy. Objects made from lead that resemble buttons are small weights used in the days of long clothing to keep skirts and coats in place. They were sewn inside the hem and sometimes became loose. Consequently as lead does not rust they are often found in old button tins or outdoors. Churchyards and shrubberies seem popular locations!

Painted metal

Tin or other metal buttons can be painted or treated with similar substances to simulate enamel or purely to add colour. When in new condition they can be attractive but damage easily with wear. Collectors are advised to beware of any button described as 'cold enamel' which is often a euphemism for paint. See also *Tin*.

Perforated

This type of hollow button was made in Czechoslovakia and Germany since the Second World War and is usually a three-piece construction. The raised front is finely perforated to allow a shiny intermediate to twinkle through. The back incorporates the shank and like the front may be finished in chrome or gilt colour. Named *twinkles* in America, these buttons are found in all European countries. In mint condition they can be attractive as cheap dress accessories.

Pewter

Pewter buttons have been made in Europe from the thirteenth century and in Britain from the fifteenth, but frequently they are rather dull heavy discs of little collector merit. In America however, from about 1790, finely designed cast pewter buttons were made in New England by at least twenty different firms. Early ones were cast complete with loop shanks in moulds making up to nine at a time. Later wire shanks were used. Once the technique of gilding brass was acquired pewter fell from favour but was revived at the turn of the century. English pewter was then used by Liberty's for their Tudric ware and buttons, often with ceramic centres, were made in limited numbers. Modern pewter buttons using thin sheet over wood moulds are generally studio productions. See also *Zinc*.

English silver

The use of silver to make decorative buttons as distinct from uniform or regalia types was a fairly short-lived fashion dating from about 1890 to 1910, but coinciding with a period of design now known as art nouveau. Boxed sets of attractive silver buttons

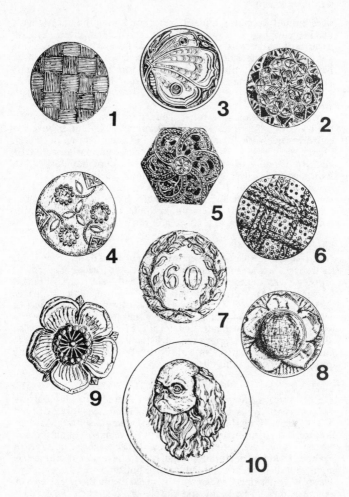

Fig. 3. METAL BUTTONS
1 and 2. British gilded brass, c. 1800; known as golden age. 3 and 4. Painted metal, c. 1920; probably European. 5 and 6. Perforated metals; Czechoslovakian, c. 1960. 7. British pewter button issued c. 1770 to 60th (Royal American) regiment of foot, which later became King's Royal Rifle Corps (S. Godsell). 8. Pewter over tin with Ruskin pottery centre; Tudric type c. 1900. 9. English silver; London, 1901, SJ. 10. English silver; Birmingham, 1908, JAR.

were initially popular until it was found that the metal badly marked clothing. This is why so many sets remain intact. English silver buttons were assayed by law and the marks include a lion passant (standing sideways). Buttons marked *stirling* are often American. Silver uniform and dress buttons are fairly frequently seen and may denote either rank or that the MFH was a snob!

Foreign silver

Many European and other countries have produced silver buttons often for their national costumes. The Dutch have excelled in this work for a long period but have also made tourist items. Their early work and that from the Scandinavian countries and Russia deserve special study. It is seldom hallmarked. In Asia low-grade silver buttons are common, being far below the British standard of 925 parts of pure silver per 1000. Small amounts of alloys are added for strength. Silver buttons are not as rare as some recent prices might indicate and are too easily equated with jewellery of a far greater intrinsic value.

Silver-plated

Fusing a thin sheet of silver to a copper base dates from 1742; the process is known as Sheffield plate. Later various methods of dipping were discovered and more recently electrolysis. Plated buttons are often from either military or civilian uniforms, particularly liveries worn by servants during the nineteenth century. The backmarks may refer either to the maker or the wholesale tailor who made the clothes. Livery buttons were also made in brass and copper and are not rare. Plated decorative buttons were a minority line and do not tarnish or mark clothing quite as easily as solid silver.

Steel

Steel buttons have been made for two hundred years and are still occasionally used on court dress. There are three distinct methods of making them. During the eighteenth century Matthew Boulton, a Birmingham craftsman, developed quality steel buttons as an alternative to highly expensive marcasite used in France. Using a perforated base plate, he inserted numerous highly polished steel rivets. This type of button is sometimes called *cut steel*. Other items were made by the same method. The earlier examples tend to be heavy and closely set, but when the fashion revived from about 1875 more open designs were used and combinations with other materials were popular. In France a M. Dauffe made a similar button about 1775 but the method of stamping sheet steel to produce a cheaper type of button was developed by a M. Trichot in 1830. Steel quickly rusts in damp climates and so was replaced by lustre glass. Flat cast steel buttons with a raised or chased design were made in small numbers. Never

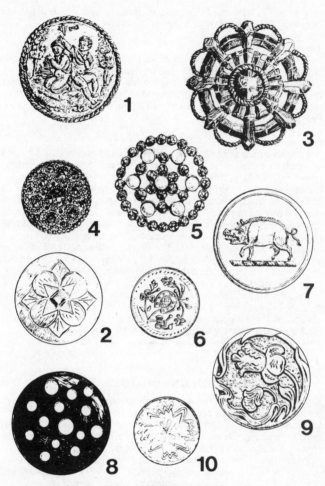

Fig. 4. METAL BUTTONS
1 and 2. Continental silver; nineteenth century. 3. Trichot-type steel button; nineteenth century. 4. Boulton-type steel button as used on British court dress. 5. Boulton-type steel with glass beads; ' te nineteenth century. 6. Silver-plated ladies' sportswear button, c. 1910; probably Irish. 7. Nineteenth-century plated livery button by Firmin's. 8 and 9. Two-piece pressed tin buttons; early twentieth century. 10. Eighteenth-century turned zinc (tombac); British.

very popular, they date from the eighteenth century and like all steel objects respond to a magnet.

Tin

Tin and tin alloys have been widely used for mass-produced buttons. They are generally modern and come from Austria, Germany and Czechoslovakia, but other countries also produced their share of these cheap and cheerful dress-trade items. Tin can be painted or plated but rusts easily and wears badly. See also *Painted metal*.

Zinc (tombac)

Buttons which are called zinc in Britain and tombac in America are usually made from an alloy of zinc and copper. The name *tombac* is of Malayan origin. Such buttons have been made since the seventeenth century or even earlier in Britain but are often difficult to distinguish from pewter. In America they date from colonial days. They are generally cast with a raised back like early brass buttons or they may have a soldered shank. The face may be plain or engine-turned or have a hand-worked design. Some have a raised centre like a breastplate. One very popular design similar to an open rose has caused buttons of this type to be erroneously considered Tudor. This design and others have recently been copied in tin for the American haberdashery trade.

Buttons made from a slightly different alloy are referred to as *hard whites* in America and date from 1790. They are a type of pewter and include some finely worked designs made before the secrets of the brass-gilding process were acquired there.

3. Enamelled metal buttons

Enamelling, the application of finely ground glass to a prepared metal surface which is then fired by intense heat, is an ancient pre-Christian art. It appears to have been developed independently by middle eastern, Chinese and Anglo-Saxon cultures but quickly spread throughout the northern hemisphere.

Enamelled buttons generally date from either the eighteenth century or an Edwardian revival period; the latter are cheaper but because of their pretty colouring have become overvalued. Eighteenth-century enamel buttons are usually French although a very few were made in Britain. Limoges, Sevres and Paris produced beautiful buttons, generally 10p (50 cent) size, with a slightly domed face. They were painted, inset with stones, laid over gold or foils and were usually finished with a metal rim and rear shank. The good quality and depth of colour is difficult to describe but once seen they can thereafter be instantly recognised.

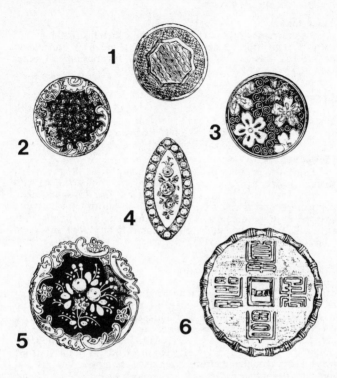

Fig. 5. ENAMELLED METAL BUTTONS
1. Basse taille; early twentieth century. 2. Champleve; French, early twentieth century. 3. Cloisonne; Japanese; late nineteenth century. 4. Emaux peint with encrusted border; French, late nineteenth century. 5. Emaux peint with champleve border; French, late nineteenth century. 6. Chinese enamelled silver; early twentieth century.

Although the various techniques of enamelling have not changed since the fifteenth century, the greatest variety was used in button making during the Edwardian period. However, just as modern enamellers seem unable to recreate Edwardian prettiness, so the Edwardians were unable to reproduce eighteenth-century quality. Small boxed sets of enamel buttons were made for the gift and tourist trades, being popular then and now.

Basse taille
This process is of Italian origin. The base metal is first engraved with an engine-turned design and then coated with transparent enamel. It was not as frequently used for buttons as other techniques.

Champleve
This is a method whereby a stamped design is filled with enamel. Coins are treated in this way. It was a very popular Edwardian method, sometimes combined with others.

Cloisonne
Particularly popular in Japan and China, this is the process of soldering wires to a base and then filling the compartments with enamel. It requires great skill to produce a fine cloisonne item, particularly one as small as a button. Such buttons are therefore scarce but were made as export items, chiefly in Japan. Occasionally foil was laid under clear enamel to produce a simulated cloisonne effect.

Emaux-peint (painted enamel)
This method was developed at Limoges during the fifteenth century and has been carried out ever since with varying degrees of skill. In the best items the domed surface was gradually built up with many layers of enamel, each independently fired, but later a production-line system was adopted and pieces of foil were incorporated to give added glitter. As with porcelain decoration, the skill of the worker is directly reflected in the quality of the finished piece. Painted enamel buttons often have champleve borders and some are decorated *en grisaille* (in monochrome). They may also be set with paste or encrusted with beads of turquoise enamel, to simulate Persian jewellery.

Paillons
This is a term used to describe items made by placing foil over several layers of enamel on an engine-turned base and then subsequently coating with further enamel. Buttons of this type are very uncommon and should not be confused with cheaper foil work. Another rarity is the *plique-a-jour* button, which is like a stained glass window or cloisonne without the base metal. They were very unpractical and their fragility alone makes them scarce.

Chinese enamel buttons made for export are often beautiful but different. Silver filigree balls partly filled with enamel, the application of transparent enamel to raised designs, tiny silver frogs on enamel lily leaves and other curiosities all come from the fertile Chinese imagination. Colouring is usually delicate and subject matter oriental and original. The Black Sea region and Russia have produced interesting, mainly cloisonne enamel buttons, but unless documented correct identification is difficult. Hearsay attributions should be regarded with caution. The enamel revival happened when the style of decoration now known as art nouveau was popular and both silver and enamel were suitable mediums for craft workers, so interesting buttons in this style are found. They were included in the specially commissioned Cymbric silverware by Liberty's of London, much of which was made by W. H. Haseler of Birmingham (see also *Pewter*). Enamelled buttons were also produced in small numbers by individuals or groups of workers in the Arts and Crafts movement, including A. E. Jones of Birmingham, who used Ruskin pottery (*q.v.*) centre pieces. Precise identification is often impossible and quality varies. In America enamel buttons were imported, but some have been made recently for the collector market.

---

4. Glass buttons

The interest in glass buttons lies in the number of techniques associated with the one basic material. In the eighteenth century glass was generally used in conjunction with other materials; in the nineteenth century it was used alone but usually with a metal shank. Wholly glass buttons with a self shank are mainly modern and are still produced, though in declining numbers. Exceptions and overlapping of styles occur, but as glass buttons (also made in sew-through designs) are seldom backmarked dating is difficult.

Italy is the oldest centre of glass button making but mass production has always been centred in Bohemia (now part of Czechoslovakia), where millions of plain and fancy buttons have been made and exported. England and France had thriving manufactories of their own from the beginning of the nineteenth century, later boosted by the presence of refugees from eastern Europe, who were also largely responsible for introducing glass button making to America.

Glass buttons, more than other types, have become subject to collector terminology in America, including several descriptions subsequently found to be erroneous and others that are rather confusing. Some of these are explained in the glossary.

Balls and domes

Ball and half-ball buttons can be made from almost any type of glass but were a nineteenth-century fashion. They were made to imitate hardstones, birds' eggs, cats' eyes or given glitter with the use of foil fragments in the mix. They were generally poured into small moulds and metal-shanked while hot and an enormous variety of colours and types exists. Their main uses were for waistcoats and children's garments, but one Birmingham maker exported large quantities to African chiefs. Neil and Tonks and J. & T. Chatwin exhibited them in 1851 and were commended for quality.

Beaded

There are two varieties of glass beaded buttons: those where small solid beads have been glued to a wood base, and those where larger hollow beads are attached to a fabric intermediate. This latter type is known as *sac a perles* in France but was not necessarily made there. The example shown came from Iran. The first type uses rather larger beads than those described under the heading *Wood*.

Crystal

Clear glass buttons are called crystal in the trade. *(Watch crystal* is an American collector's name for a type of glass-fronted button.) They may be ball-shaped, cut or moulded. Modern ones are either self-shanked or sew-throughs but lost favour with the advent of the spin drier. See also *Paste*.

Faceted

Faceted glass buttons were made by hand-cutting sheet glass before machines took over. Later the use of moulds made simulation easy. A great many black-glass imitation-jet buttons are faceted as the technique gives added brightness, but any colour glass can be treated in this way. Small faceted pieces of glass mounted on a base plate of metal, rather in the same manner as cut steel, are known as passementerie glass. They are not rare, usually black and break easily.

Foil under

Inserting foil into a moulded glass button gives added interest and was popular in Edwardian times, when matching hatpin heads and cufflinks (for ladies) were made. The Austrians specialised in a technique whereby the foil was laid in the mould before pouring the glass; it was then turned out like a capped pudding. They often used green and blue to produce a peacock eye effect. Foil was also used under clear glass in metal-mounted waistcoat buttons.

Italian (modern)

During the nineteen seventies Mercole Moretti of Venice produced a range of attractive buttons for export to America (and possibly elsewhere) using long-established Venetian styles. Some of these buttons are made from coloured glass canes set on

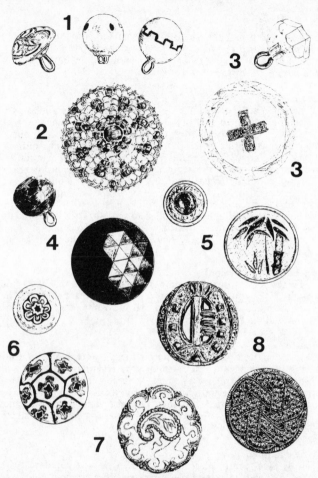

Fig. 6. GLASS BUTTONS
1. Three examples of ball and dome buttons; late nineteenth century.
2. Sac a perles glass beaded button; Iranian, twentieth century. 3.
Two examples of crystal buttons. 4. Two examples of faceted black
glass buttons. 5. Two examples of foil under glass; the smaller metal-
mounted one is of a type known as peacock eye; the other is
Japanese (M.Jones). 6. Two examples of twentieth-century Italian
glass buttons, purchased in Denver in 1974. 7. Late nineteenth-
century button with incised (outline design) decoration. 8. Two
examples of lustre-finished pressed glass buttons; late nineteenth
century.

end in patterns; others are self-shanked moulded designs resembling striped sweets and some like Venetian beads have a matt finish. Similar smaller pieces mounted as earrings have been seen in Britain.

Lustre glass

The application of metallic silver or less frequently gilt, copper or aluminium to black pressed glass buttons began in the nineteenth century as an alternative to easily rusting steel, but it has continued with modifications ever since. Old lustre buttons are usually thin and have metal shanks. They are found in all the same variety of patterns as black glass. Matching hatpin heads were made. Modern lustre buttons usually have a built-up self shank, are relatively thick and generally 1-2p (1-5 cent) size. Old ones can be any size from ¼ inch to 2½ inches (10-100 line). The lustre, a metallic liquid, was applied to the black (or occasionally dark-coloured) buttons, which were then fired in a low-temperature muffle furnace. The backs are seldom treated with lustre.

Incised (outline design)

This type of button, which may be any opaque colour, has a fine scratch-like design, made by use of a die, on the front surface. The design is filled with paint; gold, silver, white and black are predominating colours.

Mosaic

Mosaic buttons, studs and hatpin heads were made in Italy during the nineteenth century and more recently in France and China. Numerous tiny glass or stone tesserae were arranged on end within a metal shell and on a glass ground. Some were fused by firing, others cemented and then polished. They tend to depict either Roman ruins, flora or fauna and are easily damaged. Modern tourist items can be gaudy.

Metal-mounted

Using glass centre pieces to imitate jewels was popular at the end of the nineteenth century. Some large ones are now called *gay nineties* in America and at the time of their availability in Britain were considered by ladies to be common! Earlier similar types of a superior quality are in the Luckock Collection.

Moulded (modern)

When button making recommenced after the First World War, mass-produced glass buttons were generally mechanically moulded rather than finely pressed as previously. The adoption of the built-up shank reduced the time required and a wide range of

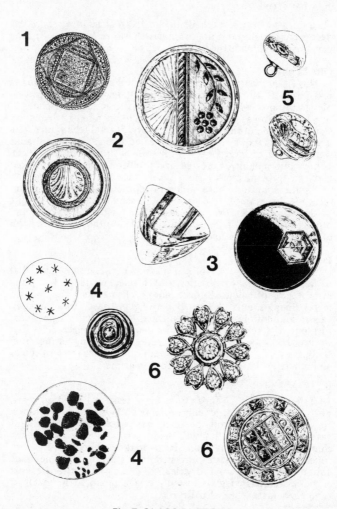

Fig. 7. GLASS BUTTONS
1. Late nineteenth-century Italian mosaic button. 2. Two examples of metal-mounted glass; late nineteenth century. 3. Two examples of 1930s moulded glass buttons. 4. Three examples of glass buttons known as old English; probably late eighteenth or early nineteenth century. 5. Two paperweight buttons; the upper one is blown and the lower cemented. 6. Two examples of paste buttons.

cheap dress buttons resulted. In the 1930s styles now called art deco were popular and the examples shown reflect this. Opaque glass and paint made the patterns. See also *Realistics*.

Old English

This type of button was made in Birmingham, the Bristol area and probably elsewhere from the end of the eighteenth century. Some appear to be 'end of the day' items from local glasshouses, but James Grove's old sample books contain nineteenth-century examples made in the Halesowen factory. Several techniques were used. Sheet glass was clipped with heated tongs; pin-head shanks were applied to large beads, while others appear to have been poured into moulds or pressed in a primitive way. Both shanked and sew-through types occur. Like American Norwalk pottery (*q.v.*), these buttons have a charm of their own. Although interesting diversities of colour occur, a semi-opaque milky white predominates. Clear varieties resembling jelly sweets are mid nineteenth-century. They were made by J. Matthews of New John Street, Birmingham, and others.

Paperweights

A button which resembles a glass paperweight is given that name. There are two varieties. Blown ones are made by fusing small pieces of coloured glass under a clear dome. They have a metal loop shank. Stuck paperweights have the coloured decoration (not always glass) cemented under a hollow glass cap, with one of several back types also cemented in place. The first variety is a superior article and generally Italian, dating from 1880; the stuck ones are east European. In America modern copies of both types have been made for collectors.

Paste

Paste has been used for buttons for at least two hundred years. Early ones are often of jewellery quality and were made in France, Italy and Britain. During the nineteenth century quality gradually gave way to glitter, but well-made versions such as Liberty-commissioned buttons and Paris-marked pieces are worth collecting. Modern paste cemented to a base is machine-made glitter that disintegrates if dry cleaned! Good paste buttons consist of pieces of faceted glass (usually clear), mounted in metal or enamelled metal. See also *Crystal*.

Pressed glass (clear) (lacy glass)

Although the technique of making pressed glass in metal moulds was developed in America during the 1840s, buttons were not produced there by this method then. Most pressed glass buttons made before the First World War came from eastern Europe. One type of very attractive button was made by pressing

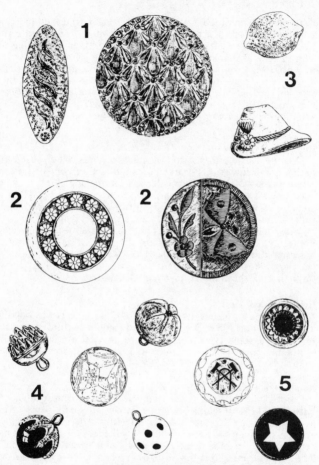

Fig. 8. GLASS BUTTONS
1. Two examples of clear pressed glass buttons with reflected decoration, sometimes known as lacy glass; European, late nineteenth century. 2. Two opaque pressed glass buttons; the right-hand one is black glass, sometimes called jet; nineteenth century. 3. Two moulded glass realistic (goofy) buttons; twentieth century. 4. Five examples of small glass buttons known as charm string types; they include a kaleidoscope in the centre, and a berry top left. 5. Three examples of fancy waistcoat buttons; the upper one is layered glass in a metal mount, the centre one c. 1880 and the lower one inlaid glass, similar to mourning buttons with a cross motif.

clear (or occasionally coloured transparent) glass and then backing it with either foil or a printed coloured pattern and coating the reverse with silver, gilt or black paint. Such buttons usually have a four-way metal shank and if round are either 10p (50 cent) or 1p (1 cent) size. Originally and erroneously thought by American collectors to come from the Sandwich Glass Co. at Boston, they were dubbed *lacy glass* after the lace-like wares made there. Never plentiful and easily damaged, they are now more easily found in Britain or Czechoslovakia than in the USA.

Pressed glass (opaque)

Opaque glass, either black or coloured, was widely used for pressing and under this heading come all the billions of buttons often misnamed 'jet', a term derived from their colour. Lustre glass (*q.v.*) is coated pressed glass. Black pressed glass made with metal dies was very fashionable during Queen Victoria's long widowhood and for several decades after her death.

A heavier type of pressed glass button, with a raised edge like a Pontefract cake, was made by the English Glass Company of Leicester during the late 1940s. The glass pieces (also used for jewellery) were cemented to a shanked back plate which may carry the name of the manufacturer or distributor.

Realistics (goofies)

Making glass buttons in the shapes of other objects was popular in the 1930s and 1950s. A wide range of colours and designs exists. In America some types are known as goofies. Similar items in synthetic materials are currently sold on haberdashery (notions) counters.

Small fancy glass (charm string)

From about 1845 to 1900 both British and European glass button makers developed a huge range of small fancy glass buttons. A nomenclature for the differing styles has developed among American collectors. Collectively the term *charm string* has been used to describe them. This refers to a craze among young ladies for collecting one thousand different small buttons, the last one being added to the string by Prince Charming. The idea originated from a newspaper competition in the 1880s and continued for some years. British makers of this type of button include G. & W. Twigg, Neal and Tonks and Smith Kemp and Wright, all of Birmingham, and James Grove of Halesowen.

Waistcoat

Fancy glass buttons were widely used on waistcoats in periods when the garment was worn. They are often interchangeable with clip fasteners and came in boxes of six. Colour and style varied

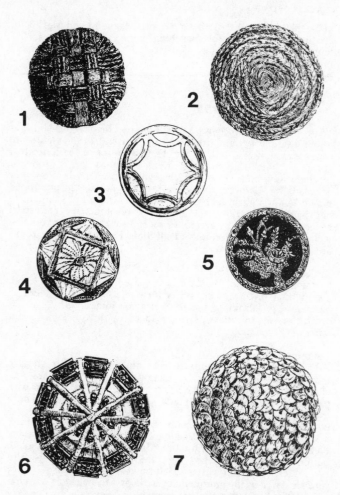

Fig. 9. FABRIC BUTTONS

1. Black braid over mould; French, twentieth century. 2. Home-made gilt braid button; probably English, early twentieth century. 3. Satin ribbon under metal shell; twentieth century. 4. Coventry woven ribbon in painted metal shell. 5. Brown velvet in metal shell with escutcheon decoration; a velvet back. 6. Beads, braid and silk combination; probably an upholstery button. 7. Brown sequins sewn over a wood mould.

and could be suited to the wearer's taste. Some were designed for evening wear, others for mourning, club affiliation, sports interest, political or religious association, and a minority denoted rather risque aspirations!

5. Fabric buttons

With notable exceptions, fabric-covered and thread buttons represent quantity rather than quality. Whereas in the eighteenth century magnificent but fragile items were made for individual garments, later billions of covered buttons were produced mechanically, until superseded by synthetic materials. Now they are made for *haute couture* garments or at home with purchased moulds on an individual basis. Although many are now mundane or shabby they represent not only revolutionary industrial processes but significant events in social history, so they should be included in any representative collection. Fabric-covered buttons are also used in upholstery.

Braided

The application of braids to a prepared base, often of wood, commenced in the nineteenth century and for certain types of garment, e.g. astrakhan, has never ceased. Some braided buttons are factory-made; others were produced by dressmakers to suit particular models.

Combinations

Fabrics have been combined with numerous other materials. Metal edges prevent wear by friction and glass enhances dull cloth. Sequins and beads covering a fabric base originated with passementerie work (*q.v.*) but later garment makers used them to liven up plain designs. Combining woven fabrics with metal was popular in the nineteenth century, particularly when Coventry woven ribbons made by the Jacquard loom method were in vogue. Pieces of ribbon with individual motifs set in the centre of a metal button within a metal shell were used to imitate enamels. Unfortunately they often rusted. Metal buttons made with pieces of velvet inserted as the intermediate are known to collectors as *velvet backs*. They are scarce in good condition. Some originally were perfumed.

Covered

The introduction in Britain of the cloth-covered or *florentine* button (named after the silk used) in 1801 caused reverberations throughout the world and was largely responsible for the subsequent decline in gilt and other metal buttons on men's civilian

1. Front and back of a seventeenth-century metal button found in Leicestershire in 1977.

2. Early eighteenth-century metal button showing engine-turned design.

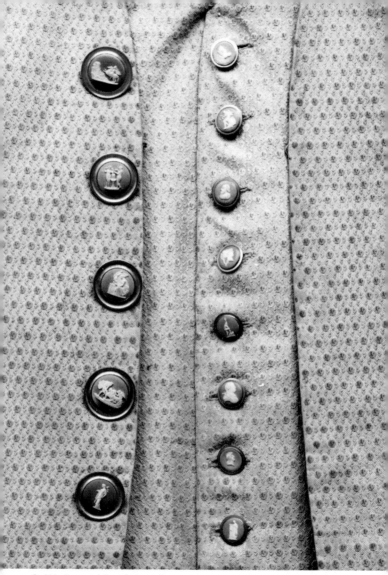

3. Wedgwood jasperware buttons on coat and waistcoat, c. 1787.

4. Eighteenth-century British buttons with metal rims, and painted decoration to imitate enamelling Luckcock Collection.

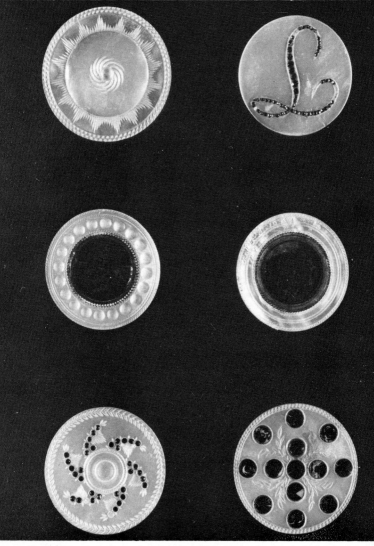

5. Eighteenth-century decorated shell buttons. Luckock Collection.

6. Eighteenth-century brass buttons of a type known as colonials in America. Luckock Collection.

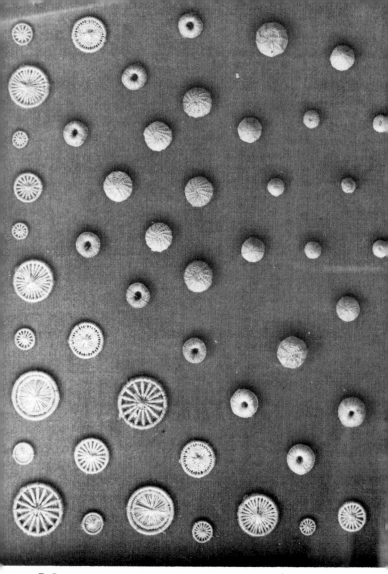

7. *Dorset thread buttons. Private collection.*

8. Nineteenth-century processed horn buttons made by James Grove and Sons, Halesowen.

9. Gilded brass, commemorative and other metal buttons from the Gaunt Collection.

10. *Archery club, workhouse and charity metal buttons from the Gaunt Collection.*

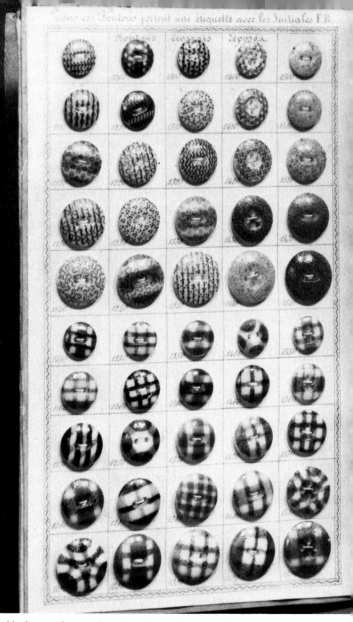

11. A page from a French salesman's sample book of pressed clay buttons, showing types now known as calicoes and ginghams.

12. *Another page from the French salesman's sample book.*

13. Small buttons c. 1880-1920 known as Austrian tinies. Author's collection.

14. A selection of buttons depicting heads arranged for an American button collectors' competition. Mrs F. Schmitte, Denver.

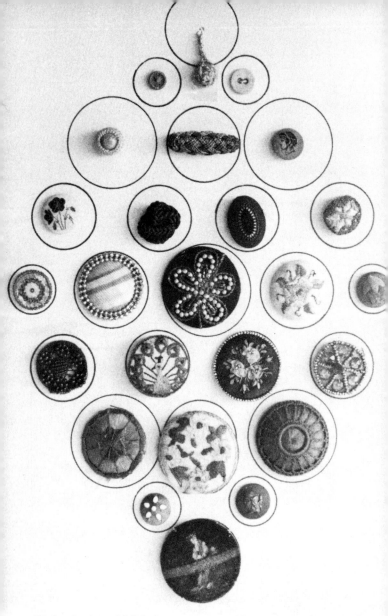

15. A selection of fabric buttons arranged for an American button collectors' competition. The late Mrs P. Sweeny, Denver.

16. Edwardian workers in a midland button factory.

17. Old shell buttons used by Mrs R. Godsell to make the Queen's Silver Jubilee motiff.

A REAL BRUMMAGEM BOY.

Published by G. Tregear, 123 Cheapside

THE MAN WOT PATRONISES THE
BUTTON MAKERS.

18. Late eighteenth-century cartoon.

wear. Benjamin Sanders, who returned to the midlands from Denmark, invented a machine which produced cloth-covered buttons using dies and pressure. He worked first in Birmingham and then in Halesowen with his son, who introduced canvas or flexible shanks to replace wire ones. Together they withstood parliamentary lobbying by metal button makers and were responsible for this type of button becoming permanent. William Elliott's 1837 patent introduced fancy covered buttons with individual centre patterns. Florentine buttons were popular throughout the nineteenth century and are still used on cassocks. Covered buttons made with woven ribbons were popular in the 1930s, some being assembled in Birmingham using ribbons from J. & J. Cash of Coventry. This firm also made a Union Jack and Queen's head design, which is periodically revived at suitable occasions. Garter buttons using ribbon and paint were made by the same method and were worn by saucy British and American ladies during the 1920s.

The utilitarian linen-covered button was the result of the invention in 1841 by Humphrey Jeffreys, a balloonist, and patenting by John Aston, of Aston's patent button-making machine. Mass production of linen buttons caused the rapid decline of the Dorset thread industry and much local hardship. Linen buttons were gradually replaced by vegetable ivory for shirts but were used for household items until after the Second World War.

Crochet

Machine and hand-worked crochet has been used as a button covering in many places, notably Ireland and France. The core may be either a wood mould or a soft substance such as kapok or wool, or in America cardboard. Hard ball-shaped buttons with loop shanks known as *French knobs* were popular with Edwardian Parisian prostitutes, which may account for their disfavour elsewhere!

Home embroidered

Decorating pieces of cloth subsequently stretched over wood or bone moulds made for the purpose began as a Victorian occupation for ladies but the later wartime scarcities caused it to continue. Magazines in the United Kingdom and USA issued instructions, and iron-on transfers could be bought. Skilled needlewomen used ribbon work, silk weaving, tatting and pillow lace in button covers, but variations of the simple stitched 'spider' predominate.

Passementerie

This term is used to describe the finely made and ornately decorated buttons produced chiefly in Italy, France and Spain during the seventeenth and eighteenth centuries. Finely embroidered fabric was laid over strong linen or silk on a wood or wire mould. It might be decorated with gold and silver wire, sequins, purl, spangles, etc. Each button was made for a specific garment, being the final elaborate adornment of a nobleman's coat, vest or breeches. Male household servants of the period often wore elaborate liveries with fine hand-worked buttons. These should not be confused with the nineteenth-century custom of decorating servants' clothes with metal crested buttons. Early passementerie buttons in good condition are now scarce.

Thread

The production of thread buttons was a cottage industry chiefly centred on Dorset, but the Leek area of Staffordshire and Scotland made more colourful examples. The buttons, usually white in Dorset, were made either by stitching over small knobs of horn or wool or by winding thread over wire rings, brought by cart from Birmingham. After carding with coloured papers to denote size, they were sold to wholesalers. A booklet on their history is now available in Lytchett Minster, once a centre of the industry. Leek buttons were made with coloured Macclesfield silks over a hard core, and in Scotland flat oval types using cotton or silk were made on the west coast.

6. Ceramic buttons

With the exception of pressed clay types, ceramic buttons have never been mass-produced. Small numbers have been made at all stages of button history. In the eighteenth century Josiah Wedgwood and others made medallions which were mounted in steel and silver. On the continent hand-painted porcelain buttons were produced in France, notably at Sevres, and at Tournai and Copenhagen.

Marked examples of nineteenth-century buttons from Meissen, Limoges, Delft, Copeland, Wedgwood and Mintons, in addition to Japanese faience (Satsuma), can be seen in major collections. Others of this period include various transfer-decorated items and from the end of the nineteenth century pottery buttons were made in several locations. Pilkington, Ruskin and Brannam are the best known. Others which are unmarked and therefore difficult to identify precisely may be modern imitations of earlier types or attempts to produce primitives.

The pressed clay process, invented in Britain but quickly transferred to France, accounts for millions of small utilitarian buttons and also attractive transfer-decorated types, which have become a collector cult in America.

Fig. 10. FABRIC BUTTONS
1. Fabric and ribbon covered garter button; British, c. 1920. 2. Woven ribbon by J. & J. Cash of Coventry; 1953. 3. Covered linen button with brass eyelets (M. Jones). 4. A florentine covered button with flexible cloth shank. 5. An eighteenth-century passementerie button. 6. A French knob — crochet silk over wood mould; late nineteenth century. 7. Black crochet over a mould; probably Irish, late nineteenth century. 8. Home-made embroidered button worked on linen over wood mould. 9. Home-made button using fine ribbon work and silk embroidery; nineteenth century.

Art pottery (American)

Pottery buttons known as Norwalk were made in several locations in Connecticut during the first half of the nineteenth century and possibly earlier. They are usually clay discs with a pin-head shank and are glazed in a variety of mottled colours similar to domestic wares produced in Bennington, Vermont (or Rye, East Sussex).

Art pottery (British)

The Royal Lancastrian pottery was built in 1892 at Clifton Junction, Manchester, by the four brothers Pilkington. It developed chiefly as a tile manufactory but during the period 1893-1915, when William Burton, formerly of Wedgwood, was chief chemist, a specialist range of finely glazed pottery was produced and small items including buttons were used initially for glaze experiments before limited production runs were made. The pottery section closed in the 1930s but the company continued as tile makers. Pilkington buttons are unmarked, but part of an authentic selection sold at Sotheby's in 1972 is now part of the present author's collection lodged in the Somerset County Museum at Taunton.

Small quantities of red clay buttons, usually with a deep royal blue glaze similar in construction to the Pilkington items and marked either *CHB*, *Brannam* or *Barum* (Latin for Barnstaple), were made at the Devon pottery of Charles H. Brannam before 1939. In the west of England similar unmarked white clay buttons with a deep emerald-green glaze also occur. They *may* have originated from the Torquay potteries.

Commercial quantities of Ruskin buttons were produced at the Smethwick pottery owned by Edward and W. Howson Taylor from 1898 to 1935. They are made from white clay and glazed in various colours. They have a distinctive shaped self shank and are backstamped *Ruskin*.

In 1896 Mary Watts, second wife of G. F. Watts, the Victorian painter and sculptor, designed a unique mortuary chapel for the village of Compton near Guildford, employing local people for the building and the decoration in art nouveau design terracotta and gesso. When the chapel was completed the workers wished to continue, so under the direction of Mrs Watts a pottery was constructed to produce commercial work. Mrs Watts, thirty years younger than her husband, died in 1938, but the pottery continued until the 1950s, producing a range of well-designed decorative objects, which were biscuit-fired and coloured with oils and tempera. In the 1920s a small range of buttons, pendants and brooch pieces was made. The products were sold locally or exported to Europe and the works was known as the Compton Art Potters Guild, using the marks *PAG* or *Compton Pottery*

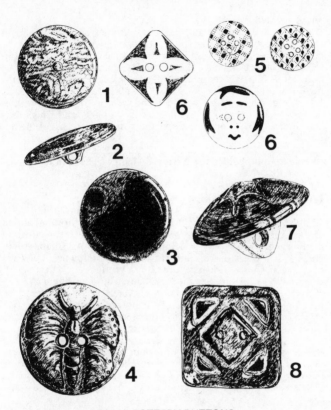

Fig. 11. POTTERY BUTTONS
1. Norwalk pottery; American, c. 1820. 2. Ruskin pottery; English, c.
1930. 3. Pilkington (Royal Lancastrian) pottery; English, c. 1904.
Brannam appears similar. 4. Watts pottery; English, c. 1925 (R.
Jeffreys). 5. Two pressed clay buttons of a type known as calicoes;
French, nineteenth century. 6. Two pressed clay buttons of a type
known as stencils; Bohemian, early twentieth century. 7 and 8.
Unknown British studio pottery; twentieth century.

Guildford. The buttons (unmarked) are sew-through types of 10p
(50 cent) size or larger, of white clay, with a raised design.
Colouring was typical of the period, orange and green
predominating. They now represent an obscure but unique type of
button. As they are unsuited to either laundering or dry cleaning
few have survived.

Hand-painted

Professionally made hand-painted buttons from the eighteenth century are highly prized by collectors. They are generally of continental origin and were bespoke for specific clients, being 10p (50 cent) size or larger. They include rebus buttons where the decoration is partly letters and partly objects representing puns made to humour Gallic lovers. An English form of this idea is found in children's puzzles. Nineteenth-century painted porcelain buttons made for tourists sometimes lack quality and finish, but good items came from the Copeland, Minton and Meissen factories.

Amateur decorating of button blanks supplied for the purpose was an indoor hobby for Victorian ladies. The quality of the finished item varies.

Pressed clay (small chinas)

Pressed clay buttons were the result of an invention, later adapted to tile making, by Richard Prosser of Birmingham in 1840. Initially the buttons, made by pressing dry clay dust in moulds, were produced by Minton and Boyle, W. Chamberlain and Co. of Worcester and some Birmingham companies, but from about 1855 the French took over mass production. The firm of Bapertrosses of Braire was the main source but later the technique moved to Bohemia and possibly America where they are thoroughly documented. Some of them were underglaze transfer-printed with patterns similar to contemporary calico prints, others checkered like ginghams or printed with stencilled designs. There is a wide range of shapes and sizes. *Agate* and *carnelian* were British manufacturers' terms to denote whether the buttons were made from earthenware or porcelain. The majority of small china buttons found in Britain now are either white or plain colours, shirt size or smaller. Production ceased between the world wars.

Satsuma

This is the name given to Japanese earthenware or faience made originally from the fifteenth century by Koreans resettled in Nawashirogawa, Kyushu. During the nineteenth century an export variety was produced at Ota, also in Satsuma province, and many items, including buttons, were made specifically for western markets. The earlier buttons are generally finely decorated with flora, fauna or scenic subjects outlined in gold on a cream ground and may be marked with either characters or a cross within a circle. Later types frequently have a heavy blue border and depict geisha girls, samurai or more coarsely executed designs. Since the mid 1960s modern reproductions have been exported to America. The body of these is generally whiter and the colours are more garish than those of the older buttons, which come in numerous

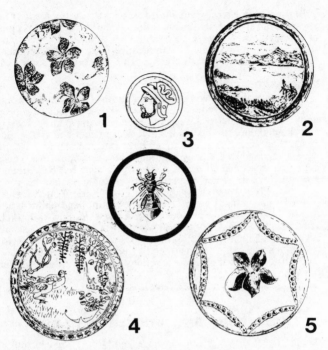

Fig. 12. CERAMIC BUTTONS
1. Transfer-printed; probably European, c. 1910. 2. Amateur painting on a ceramic blank; British, c. 1890. 3. Two examples of transfer-printed porcelain in metal mounts; probably French, nineteenth century (sometimes known as Liverpool transfers). 4. Japanese faience or Satsuma ware; late nineteenth century. 5. Hand-painted porcelain from a large set; probably French, late nineteenth century (R. Godsell).

sizes and several shapes. Hatpin heads (flat or ball-shaped), brooches and buckle pieces were also made.

Studio
 During the 1930s several small British potteries produced buttons, initially to meet a fashion craze and later to combat mass-produced mediocrity. Such buttons tend to be rather too heavy for modern clothing and have curiosity, rather than intrinsic, value.

In America the term *studio button* signifies a button made from any material specifically for the collector market. Some are copies of antiques, others merely the producer's whim. Quality varies and some types have no practical application. Early limited editions now fetch surprisingly high prices when collections are auctioned.

Transfer

Small metal-mounted porcelain buttons with monochrome transfer decoration frequently depicting classical heads have been wrongly attributed to Liverpool, because American collectors associated them with the Saddler and Green manufactory of about 1750. These buttons are of a much later date and almost certainly were assembled in Paris using French-made components. Those depicting insects or birds and some with a coloured background are rare, but all are more frequently seen in Britain than in America. From about 1875 until the First World War transfer-printed bone-china buttons, sometimes with hand-painted additions, were produced quite widely for the tourist market. Limoges, Paris, modern Capo di Monte, the Thuringian German factories and Vienna are all probably sources, but the buttons are seldom marked. Many were originally sold as boxed sets, the name on the box being that of the local retailer. Some are of very inferior quality.

7. Horn, bone and wooden buttons

These three natural substances have jointly been used in button making almost continuously from the seventeenth century, but the periods of their individual popularity have varied. Moulded horn buttons were a nineteenth-century product, while wood was popular between the wars, followed by a fashion for natural horn. Bone, used in great quantities during the eighteenth and early nineteenth centuries, was gradually replaced by other materials.

Bone

Bone buttons, the mainstay of peasant clothing before 1875, were made all over the British Isles in small local manufactories, and production was not centred on one area. Even some quite small villages had a local button maker, who used rib and shin bones from sheep and cattle, which were cut, turned and drilled to make simple buttons. Larger concerns, which often also made horn buttons, worked on a production-line basis. Buttons were often dyed dark brown. They acquire an attractive patina with age and may wear unevenly. Occasionally an owner or maker pricked an initial or symbol on the back of the button with a heated needle but generally they are unmarked.

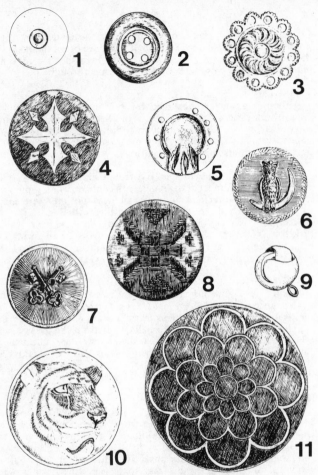

Fig. 13. HORN AND BONE BUTTONS
1. Turned bone with pin-head shank; British, nineteenth century. 2. Turned bone dyed brown; British, nineteenth century. 3. Carved bone; British, nineteenth century (R. Godsell). 4. Natural horn inlaid with pieces of shell; British, nineteenth century. 5. Turned natural horn with brass studs; British, nineteenth century. 6. Modern die-stamped natural horn imitating earlier style; British. 7 and 8. Dyed horn die-stamped; British, nineteenth century. 9. Carved ivory; probably Chinese, nineteenth century. 10. Engraved design on ivory; probably Japanese, early twentieth century (M. Jones). 11. Inlaid tortoiseshell; probably French, nineteenth century (M. Jones).

Carved bone buttons, often in flower-head designs, were popular on children's wear and sometimes have brass shanks. Like the sew-through types, they can be distinguished from other materials by the tiny dark flecks occurring throughout.

Tusk ivory

Although an ideal substance for button making, ivory has always been expensive and scarce. It has been used in two distinct ways. During the eighteenth century thin sheets of ivory were hand-painted in Europe and then mounted under glass after the manner of miniatures. Such buttons, now scarce, have been imitated.

Carved ivory buttons come mainly from China, Japan and Italy. The better ones date from the nineteenth century, when some were inlaid with semi-precious stones. Later ivory buttons were made for tourists and had scratched designs infilled with dye.

Alaskan Eskimos have also made ivory buttons from walrus tusk for American collectors and tourists. Ivory in all forms has been frequently imitated even with synthetic materials and the term is sometimes loosely used to refer to vegetable ivory (*q.v.*).

Tortoiseshell

During the eighteenth and nineteenth centuries fine buttons, studs and hatpin heads were made from tortoiseshell, but in very limited numbers. Recent items with a similar appearance are usually imitations. True tortoiseshell comes from the great hawk-billed sea turtle and can be polished to show fine gradations of colour. Buttons were often inlaid with metals, paste or shell pieces and were produced in France, Italy and Germany, rarely in Britain, but not in America.

Horn

Horn buttons are of two distinct types: processed or moulded horn from hoofs, and natural horn from antlers and head horns. During the nineteenth century millions of buttons were made in the Birmingham area by softening hoof horn with heat, dyeing it and then die-stamping buttons. The quality of the button depended on that of the die and some very fine designs were produced mainly in black, but red, green, brown and the natural colour also occur. Many horn buttons are backmarked. T. Cox, T. W. Ingram and James Grove were major producers. Processed horn can be distinguished from other materials by the pick mark left in the back by a pin-like tool used to lift the hot button from its mould. Hoof-horn buttons were also made in France, often marked *Depose* or *Bassot*, after Emile Bassot, who introduced the embedded wire shank, quickly copied by British makers. Some military buttons were made in black horn until the 1950s but now synthetic substances are used.

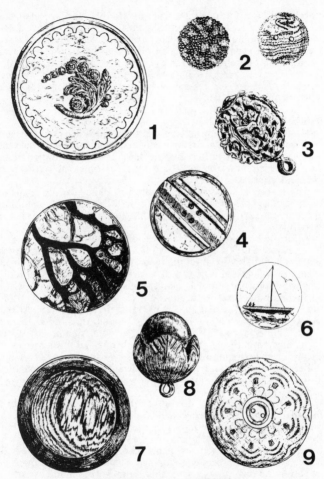

Fig. 14. WOODEN BUTTONS
1. Wood veneer in metal shell with escutcheon decoration; European, c. 1910. 2. Two examples of glass beading on wood; 1930s. 3. Chinese cupressus nut in metal mount; late nineteenth century. 4. Coconut shell reversed; German, 1935 (Gans Collection). 5. Machine marbling on wood; 1920s. 6. Hand-painting on beech wood; twentieth century. 7. Inlaid woods by Rademacher of Berlin, c. 1930 (Gans Collection). 8. Hand-carved mahogany. 9. Machine-turned wood; Bohemia, 1930s (Gans Collection).

Natural horn buttons date from about 1850 and are made by either slicing deer antlers or cutting buffalo horn into strips from which button blanks are stamped, turned, polished and drilled. In the nineteenth century Austria and Bavaria were the main centres of trade, but more recently James Grove and other British makers have made natural horn buttons, popular with leather clothes. There has also been a small local trade in Scottish stag-horn buttons for a long period.

Wood

Varieties of wooden button occur worldwide, but few are universal in type or age. Being easily available and easily worked, wood is a medium button makers have often used either when learning their craft or as a substitute in times of natural or political crisis.

The coating of wooden buttons with fine glass beading seems to have been a short-lived innovation of the 1930s. In mint condition they are attractive but they wear badly. They were made in Bohemia.

After the First World War ivory, bone and shell were scarce in Germany and later, owing to political pressures, Jewish button makers had difficulty obtaining good materials, so some of them turned to woods and used a wide variety to produce fine buttons. These were turned, carved, inlaid, veneered, etc. Rademacher, a former cabinet maker, produced excellent buttons for Adolf Gans, a Berlin distributor. Others were made for Alfred Schweitzer, a Berlin wholesaler, from thuja tree roots, carved ebony and macassa woods. Cheaper machine-made items originated from Silesia (Poland) and Bohemia. Thin wood veneers sandwiched between metal mounts are referred to by American collectors as *wood backs*. They are Edwardian and were made in Europe, as were imitation hand-carved buttons from glue and sawdust pressed in moulds.

Primitive people have often used drilled nuts as buttons, but mounted *Cupressus funebris* and similar nuts come from China. Similar-shaped metal buttons were used on Chinese costume, but the nut button and bead seem to have been made for Edwardian tourists from a tree frequently planted near temples. Coconut shell has been used to produce quaintly shaped gimmick buttons wherever the nuts grow, but quality buttons were made by Adolf Gans in the 1930s using discarded coconut shell from the Stollwerk chocolate factory in Berlin. By using the reverse side a two-tone effect was achieved. Vegetable ivory buttons (*q.v.*) are sometimes called 'nut' buttons in the trade.

Painted wood buttons were briefly popular during the 1930s and then again after the Second World War, when other materials were scarce. Heat and pressure were used to make raised designs. Germany, Austria and Czechoslovakia were the main sources.

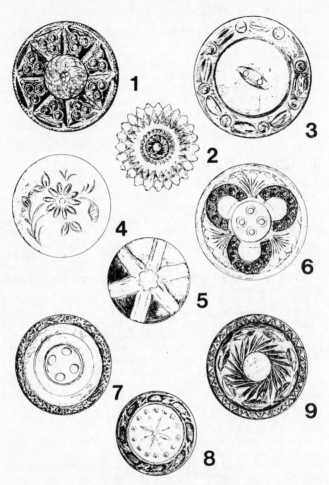

Fig. 15. SHELL BUTTONS

1. Machine-carved white and smoked combination; British, nineteenth century. 2. Eighteenth-century hand-carved shell with paste centre; British. 3. Machine carving on tinted shell; twentieth century. 4. Hand engraving on gold iridescent shell; nineteenth century. 5. Surface-dyed shell with machine cutting; early twentieth century. 6. White shell set with steel studs; British, nineteenth century. 7. Tinted shell with brass rim; probably American, late nineteenth century. 8 and 9. Two-piece metal buttons with shell centres; early twentieth century.

Turned wood buttons may be locally made as many small firms used woods, but hardwood items of quality are frequently Irish, for during the early part of this century firms in both Dublin and Cork specialised in wooden buttons, smaller and less complex than the German types. In 1851 William Griffiths of Dublin displayed bog-oak buttons at the Great Exhibition. This trade continued for some time and the buttons are easily mistaken for jet. The Irish still make wooden buttons to wear with Aran knits.

8. Shell buttons

Buttons made from a variety of mollusc shells, often called pearl or mother-of-pearl, were mass-produced in the Birmingham area from the beginning of the nineteenth century and in America from 1885. They were also made in Europe and the Far East. Fine buttons using shell, either alone or in conjunction with other materials, were made at a much earlier date on a more individual basis. Examples of these are in the Luckcock, Rothschild and D'Allemagne collections. There is also a story told that George Washington obtained conch-shell buttons made in Hartford, Connecticut, from a Baron Steuben.

The shells used in button making were imported from the Pacific, Indian Ocean and Red Sea. Availability and price governed the type used at any particular time and, once made up, the original type of shell used is almost impossible to discern. Black (grey) or smoked pearl buttons were not popular before the 1850s; the dark areas of shell had previously been discarded or used for knife handles. In America from 1890 utilitarian buttons were made from fresh-water shells found in the Mississippi and other major rivers. Californian abalone shell was used in a small way. This is of the same family as the Guernsey ormer occasionally used in French buttons. Carved cowrie-shell buttons from Italy are now rare but attractive.

From the time of the Great Exhibition shell buttons set in metal mounts became popular. Other varieties include those set with steel studs, those painted with silver or gold leaf and those of shell used with other materials. The bulk of production, however, has always been the shirt and pyjama type with two or four holes. Fancy carved shell buttons were constantly popular but always expensive.

Shell buttons are still made on a reduced scale, chiefly in Asia, and finished with a stuck plastic back piece. In Jordan a range of fancy carved shell buttons has been created for the American collector market by people who also make pendants, etc.

Ordinary sew-through shell buttons have been used for decorating clothing and artifacts by people of various cultures.

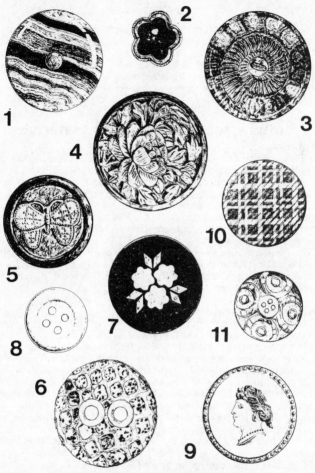

Fig. 16. MISCELLANEOUS MATERIALS
1. Agate with pin-head shank; nineteenth century. 2. Bloodstone waistcoat button mounted in rolled gold; nineteenth century. 3. Rear view of button made from a polished ammonite (R. Godsell). 4. Cinnabar button; late nineteenth century. 5. Leather button with lugged metal butterfly; c. 1920s. 6. Snakeskin over wood mould with casein eyelets; c. 1935 (Gans Collection). 7. Papier-mache inlaid with shell chips; nineteenth century. 8. Rubber liberty bodice button (M. Jones). 9. Goodyear hard rubber button; American, nineteenth century. 10. Stencil-decorated vegetable ivory button; early twentieth century. 11. Turned vegetable ivory.

63

The London costermonger with his 'pearly' outfit is well known. Less so are the button blankets made by north-west coast American Indians using buttons received in trade with the Chinese; and decorated skirts and caps are found in Africa. Button decoration is also known among Australian aborigines.

9. Buttons made from other materials

Papier-mache

This substance was invented in France but developed in England in the mid eighteenth century. Pulped paper was mixed with a binding agent and set in moulds before being varnished black to imitate oriental lacquer — hence the term japanning. Buttons were among objects made by Henry Clay of Birmingham, who patented a heat-resisting method in 1772, but those inlaid with mother-of-pearl are more common and date from 1825, when the process was patented by Jennens and Betteridge, successors to Clay. Similar buttons were made in France during the nineteenth century. Others were decorated with tartan designs but should not be confused with Mauchline ware, in which printed paper was glued to a wood mould.

Minerals (hardstone)

Numerous mineral substances have been used to produce buttons, often locally. During the nineteenth century quartz-pebble polishing was popular and buttons were also made in the Middle East by embedding turquoise chips in resin and mounting in a metal shell. Mineral waistcoat buttons were made in Birmingham, often using stones from Bohemia. The Chinese exported jade buttons, the Italians lapis lazuli and cameos cut from lava and marble. Mineral buttons are often set in gold or silver or inlaid. True jet was seldom used for button making, being basically unsuitable and scarce. Nearly all the so-called 'jet' buttons are black glass or some other material named after their colour.

Cinnabar is the name given by the Chinese to a mixture of ore of mercury and red lac. A base material, often wood, is coated with the mix, which hardens as it dries, and can then be carved.

Many other minerals and related substances have been used in a small way and assembling a collection is particularly interesting for the amateur geologist.

Leather and fur

Buttons made of plaited thonging are used on leather garments and in the middle ages flat leather disc buttons, similar to mattress buttons, were used. Decorative leather work is generally

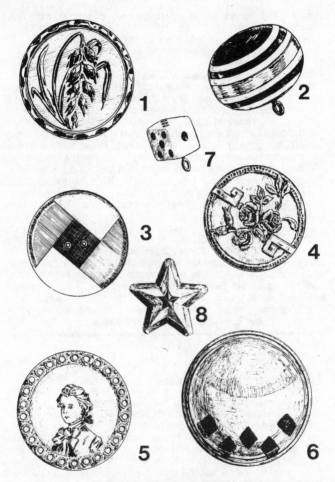

Fig. 17. SYNTHETIC BUTTONS
1. Bakelite; late nineteenth century. 2. Two pieces of laminated casein with metal-covered joint; European, 1930s. 3. Veneered casein; European, 1930s. 4. Sheet celluloid in metal shell; European, late nineteenth century. 5. Printed portrait under celluloid with a metal mount; sometimes known as a lithograph; European, early twentieth century (R. Godsell). 6. Hollow sheet celluloid; 1920s. 7. Modern synthetic button purchased in America, 1975. 8. Laminated casein star from victory celebrations, 1945 (R. Godsell).

modern, but leather has been successfully combined with other materials for some time. Snake and other fine skins stretched over wood moulds date from between the wars. Fur buttons, usually for fur garments, were popular at the same time.

Corozo or dum nut (vegetable ivory)

Buttons made from corozo or dum nuts, the fruit of the tagua palm, were mass-produced from the mid nineteenth century and almost wholly replaced bone for utilitarian purposes in Britain, Europe and America. Later they were superseded by synthetic substances. The nuts originated in South America and Africa, initially being used as ballast in Spanish ships, but once their potential was known specific cargoes were collected. After removal of the outer husk, the kernel was sliced and buttons made by stamping or turning. Dyeing was difficult owing to the dense nature of the material and so was generally superficial and often faded. Millions of these buttons were made in their day, but large ones are scarce.

A report on child labour issued in 1864 tells a sad story of the Birmingham button trade, although it was no worse than other industries of the time. Pauper boys were employed at 'cobbers' (nut crackers), working long hours in appalling conditions, while little girls acted as 'putters in' to women press operatives. Some factory owners did their best for their workers, but competition was keen and profits low. Many of the firms visited made vegetable ivory buttons and included William Aston, Smith & Wright, J. Cope, E. Lepper and Thomas Bullock and Sons.

10. Synthetic buttons

The vast majority of modern buttons are made from materials loosely referred to as plastic. Very few of them are likely ever to have collector interest, although for the benefit of posterity perhaps examples should be retained in major collections. Plastic or composition substances were introduced during the last years of the nineteenth century, initially as attempts to produce synthetic substitutes for scarce natural materials, such as jet and tusk ivory. American manufacturers played a leading role in early developments, but European production was revolutionised by the German use of casein between the two world wars.

Bakelite

This material, frequently seen in older electrical fittings, was invented in 1908 by Dr Leo Hendrick Baekeland, a Belgian living in America. Bakelite was used to make buttons, brooches and

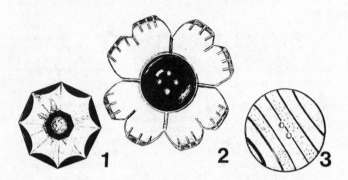

Fig. 18. SYNTHETIC BUTTONS
1. Perspex with painted design and paste centre. 2. Plexiglass with cemented casein centre. 3. Laminated synthetic resin with intrusions. All German, 1930s (Gans Collection).

bracelets as one of the many jet imitations. The buttons, now fairly scarce, often have fine-quality raised decoration.

Casein

Although the chemical process of setting casein, the coagulant in milk, was discovered in 1903, it was not until after the First World War that it was used in button making. Pioneers in this field were the Internationale Galalith Gesellschaft in Hamburg, Germany. They made buttons not only from sheet casein by turning, milling, laminating or pressing, but also from carved and turned casein rod to produce ball and half-ball buttons. Casein is capable of taking only a surface dye. This fact was used by Galalith to produce decorative and interesting effects between the two wars, when large bright 'plastic' buttons were popular. Other manufacturers quickly took up the material, which has now been largely replaced by other synthetics.

Celluloid

Celluloid was invented in 1869 by John W. Hyatt of New Jersey as an ivory imitation. Its first use was for billiard balls. There are two distinct types of celluloid button, in addition to the use of clear celluloid to replace glass. The late nineteenth-century type of button used sheet celluloid (often ivory colour) in conjunction with metal, paste and sequins to produce shanked buttons that imitate eighteenth-century designs. They are often 10p (50 cent) size and, when in good condition, attractive. They were made in Europe and America.

Between the world wars a different type of hollow domed celluloid button was made by enclosing the edges of concave sheet celluloid between a metal backplate with a cut-out shank and a wood intermediate. The celluloid might be either opaque or transparent. A glitter effect was created by using clear celluloid over tinfoil attached to the intermediate. These buttons are often large and rather vulgar in design. They are plentiful in old English button boxes, for as celluloid is highly inflammable button makers in both Britain and America were compelled to cease production following serious fires. This type therefore quickly lost favour.

Pieces of clear celluloid often replaced glass in both decorative waistcoat buttons and a larger type sometimes referred to by collectors as a *lithograph*. A coloured printed picture was used in combination with a metal shell and celluloid to produce a cheap copy of an eighteenth-century hand painting under glass. Lithograph buttons are Edwardian or later and have no intrinsic value.

Composition

A wide variety of substances ranging from wood shavings and glue to powdered metal and shellac are referred to as composition. Buttons made from such substances are difficult to identify accurately without documentation. Some of them were made locally, using materials which happened to be available at the time. After the First World War a German firm in Troisdorf, Rheinland, made imitation horn buttons from the waste products of ammunition known as venditor. These academically interesting buttons have a waxy surface and are backmarked *Germany*.

Modern synthetic materials

It is outside the scope of this book to discuss modern synthetic substances, which are numerous, but perhaps collectors may be reminded that clever imitations in synthetic materials have deceived not a few! Lightness, mould lines and melting in hot water or benzine are indications that a button may be made from a synthetic substance.

Perspex, plexiglass and synthetic resin

These materials were used in Germany and elsewhere in the inter-war period. Although originally clear, plexiglass undergoes a chemical change with age, turning yellow. It requires expert chemical knowledge to distinguish it from synthetic resin when the provenance of the article is unknown. Metal intrusions were often used with resin to produce a glittery effect. Perspex buttons are sometimes referred to as aeroplane glass, as early aircraft windows

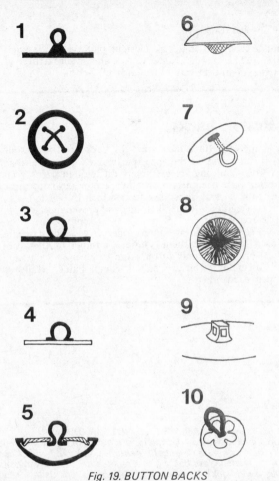

Fig. 19. BUTTON BACKS

1. Cone shank, metal; pre nineteenth century (tombac) (see also plate 1). 2. Crossed catgut loops, metal sheet over wood mould; usually pre nineteenth century. 3. Alpha-type shank, metal; from 1800. 4. Omega-type shank, metal; from 1800. 5. Sanders construction, metal; from 1802. 6. Flexible cloth shank; from 1825 (see also fig. 10, no. 4). 7. Pin-head shank, various materials; from seventeenth century (see also fig. 13 no. 1). 8. Thread back, cloth or combination; from sixteenth century to about 1930. 9. Metal-box four-way metal shank usually on glass; nineteenth or early twentieth century (see also fig. 6 no. 1) (applied birdcage). 10. Metal loop shank with rosette back-plate, generally on glass; nineteenth and early twentieth century (rosette back).

were made from this material. Designs painted on the back are magnified when viewed frontally. A major manufacturer of all three types of button was Marquardt of Berlin.

11. Button backs

As far as the collector is concerned the back of a button can be nearly as important as the face, particularly if it is a shanked variety. Many buttons are extremely difficult to date precisely; others often have deceptive decoration. Examination of the back often reveals the true substance from which the button is made and can give a guide as to its likely age and provenance.

The diagrams on pages 69 and 71 show some of the different backs a collector might encounter, together with the names most often used to describe them. Quite a number of these are of American origin and may differ from those used by manufacturers. The dates given are only a rough guide. Many styles overlapped each other.

Opposite page: Fig. 20. BUTTON BACKS
11. Loop shank with metal backplate, often on glass; many variations occur; nineteenth and twentieth centuries. 12. Embedded metal shank with swirled glass back, glass; nineteenth and early twentieth centuries (swirl back). 13. Built-up self shank of type usually seen in glass; twentieth century. 14. Whistle construction, vegetable ivory, pressed clay, compositions, etc; variations known; mid nineteenth to early twentieth century. 15. Self shank of type usually seen in pottery or porcelain; from late nineteenth century (similar style found on modern pressed metals). 16. Three examples of modern metal shanks; usually after Second World War. 17. Two examples of modern metal cut-out shanks; usually after First World War. 18. Detail of modern synthetic shank with thread guide; may be in one or two pieces, stuck, moulded or pressed. 19. Fisheye; nineteenth-century shell and many modern buttons. 20. A stud back and glass hatpin-head back — items frequently confused with buttons; generally c. 1880-1920.

11

12

13

14

15

16

17

18

19

20

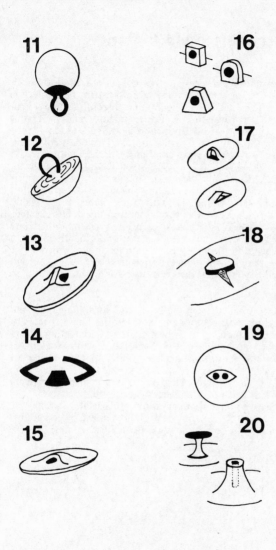

12. Where to see old buttons

It is not easy to see representative collections of buttons in Britain: few are on public display as interest in the subject is fairly recent. The Luckock Collection (eighteenth century) is in Birmingham City Museum, as is the mainly military Gaunt Collection. The Rothschild Collection is at Waddesdon Manor in the care of the National Trust. Primrose Peacock's collection including the Gans (inter-war years) and Heatherington (livery) selections is on loan to the Somerset County Museum in Taunton but may only be seen in its entirety by prior appointment. Many other museums have small numbers of buttons either on costume or with other items of the same material; for example, Dorset thread buttons are in Dorchester.

It is always advisable to make a prior appointment at any museum if one wishes to see specific items or discuss them with a specialist. The author *does not* have buttons on public display or for sale at either her residence or business addresses but will answer specific questions if directed (with s.a.e.) via the museum in Taunton.

In Europe many major museums have small selections of buttons, but captions are usually in the local language and English-speaking staff seldom available. In the United States of America access to collections is best gained by contacting a state button society affiliated to the National Button Society of America. Several major museums, including the Cooper-Hewitt and Metropolitan Museum of Art in New York and the Smithsonian in Washington DC, have good collections but an appointment made well in advance is essential.

Readers are reminded that valuations are a salable commodity and are only worthwhile for good quality intact period items. Buttons found by excavation have no collector value.

Glossary

This glossary contains terms not explained in the main text. American collector terms are indicated by the letters (US).

Alpha shank: a brazed wire loop shank with the ends meeting centrally.

Antiquarian (US): one type of old English glass button with loop shank.

Aristocrat (US): a type of incised black glass button.

Backmark: any inscription or trade mark on the back of a button.

Birdcage (US): a two-piece clay button with cage-like back.

Brevete: French term for patented.

Bull's eye (US): a pressed clay button marked with coloured rings.

Button stick: a split wood or brass gadget used when cleaning uniform buttons.

Calico (US): a pressed clay button printed to resemble calico.

Coronet (US): a small glass button with raised beads on the front.

Depose: a French term for registered trademark.

Diminutive (US): a button ⅜ inch (15 line) or smaller.

Drum (US): a thick straight-sided button, usually American.

Eglomise: reverse painting on glass, usually eighteenth century.

Escutcheon: a metal decoration on the face of a button attached by prongs or the shank pin.

Fish eye: a two-hole button with an oval depression in the centre.

Gingham (US): a pressed clay button printed in a checkered pattern.

Habitat: buttons with botanical or zoological fragments mounted under glass, usually eighteenth century. No connection with the British firm of the same name.

Hallmark: a quality mark stamped on gold and silver items.

Hightop: a variety of Dorset button.

Kaleidoscope (US): a small glass button with applied rear design showing through.

Link button: a button similar to a cape fastening.

Mirror back: a mirror glass button, usually with metal back plate.

Omega shank: a metal loop shank with the ends bent out to resemble the Greek letter.

Pants button (US): a trouser brace or fly button, often with the tailor's name.

Paris back (US): a button backmarked *Paris*, or a Paris company.

Peacock eye (US): a type of foil-under-glass button.

Picture button (US): a metal button with a picture or object on the face.

Reflector (US): a mirror back.

Registration mark: indication of registration of British patent, usually a lozenge-shaped device.

Sew-through: a button with holes through for sewing. In the USA *sew-thru*.

Small china (US): a Prosser patent pressed clay button.

Vest button (US): a waistcoat button.

Whistle (US): a button with one hole on the front and two at the back. Usually vegetable ivory or clay.

Bibliography

Bright, M. *Buttony, the Dorset Heritage.* Lytchett Minster, 1971.

Connecticut State Button Society. *Connecticut History of Button Making.* 1976.

Great Exhibition, 1851. Official descriptive and illustrated catalogue.

Horney, Ford G. *The Button Collector's History.* Privately published, 1943.

Houart, V. *Buttons — A Collector's Guide.* Souvenir Press, 1977.

Jones, W. U. *The Button Industry.* Pitman, 1924.

Just Buttons Magazine. Southington, Connecticut, 1970-8.

Laver, J. *A Concise History of Costume.* Thames & Hudson, 1969.

Luscomb, S. *Collector's Encyclopaedia of Buttons.* Crown, 1967.

National Button Society of America. *Guidelines for Collecting China Buttons.* 1970.

Nevison, J. 'Buttons and buttonholes in the fourteenth century'. *Costume* (Journal of the Costume Society) 11, 1977.

Peacock, P. *Buttons for the Collector.* David & Charles, 1972.

Smith, Albert and Kent. *Complete Button Book.* Doubleday, 1949.

White, D. 'The Birmingham button industry'. *Journal of the Society for Post Medieval Archaeology,* 1977.

Index